THE LOWLY MAIDEN'S LOYALTY

BARBARA COOMB AND LAWRENCE TRENT

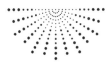

ROSIE SWAN

PUREREAD.COM

1

UP IN THE SKY

Tinkle, tinkle, crash!

"I'm sorry," three-year-old Barbara Foster cowered in the corner, covering her small head and waiting for the blow to come. Like every child her age, colourful things dazzled her, and she couldn't help herself. This particular house was full of beautiful things just calling out to her plump little hands to grab, and her pudgy little fingers just couldn't resist. "I'm sorry," she sobbed, putting her head on her raised knees.

"Come here, Child," the gentleness in the voice that came from the woman standing over her surprised her, but she held back. "Barbara, no one will hurt you; look at me," and the child did. The woman moved away and sat down on a chair, never breaking eye contact with Barbara. "Come here," Edna Coomb held out both arms, and finally the little girl moved and ran to her. "Oh Baby, you have a long way to go before you can trust people again," Edna's voice was soothing, and she picked the child up. "Go to sleep now, Little One, no one will ever hurt you again."

"Gramama," Barbara murmured sleepily and was soon fast asleep in the middle-aged woman's warm embrace. As her eyes closed in sleep, all Barbara could think about was that this nice woman smelled like roses and cinnamon buns like the ones she'd tasted before.

"Poor child," Edna's eyes filled with tears. This child had been through so much in just six months. She only wished she had known about her before today. "Oh Ingrid, why did you put me in this situation?" Edna murmured, holding the child close. "Why didn't you tell me you were so sick? I would have come in earlier and stopped Little Barbara from going through all the pain and torture she was subjected to by those you trusted to care for her."

This was her friend's grandchild she'd just rescued from Ingrid's former housekeeper and her husband, who had kept her locked up in the cellar of their house because they claimed she was too destructive. If not for Ingrid's faithful lawyer, Edna would never have found out about her friend's death and then the child.

Heavy footsteps sounded in the hallway and a thickset man of about thirty put his head into the room and then gasped, his whole body following. "Mother, what happened here? Janice will have a fit. Who did this?" He stared down at the broken shards of a beautiful vase in dismay. "This vase was given to her by her mother, and now it's all shattered."

"Would you lower your voice, Gilbert? The child is finally asleep," Edna's eyes softened as she glanced down at the sleeping child. "Poor lamb doesn't seem to have had a good night's sleep ever since Ingrid fell seriously ill and could no longer take care of her."

"Mother, who is this child and what is she doing here? And who is Ingrid?"

"Gilbert, I'll get very cross with you if your unnecessary hollering wakes this child up. Now, go and get that wife of yours to prepare the room next to mine, for that is where this little beauty will stay."

"Janice won't like this at all."

"If Janice doesn't like this, then you can both move to the cottage at the edge of the estate and live there, for after all, that's more suitable to a woman of her class, isn't it?" Edna scowled, "I asked you not to marry that woman, but you claimed to be in love and went after a person who has no social graces at all. The bane of my life!" She muttered under her breath but clearly her son heard her for his face turned red.

"Mother!"

"This house is mine and so is the money you and your scatterbrain wife are enjoying so freely. That woman does nothing but go shopping for hats and new dresses at every chance she gets. I know that she's even using the housekeeping money I allocated her to indulge her foolish tastes. If you feel that you don't want to live here with me," Edna raised her shoulders, "feel free to move into the cottage at once, and if you do so, I'll expect you to pay me rent like all the other tenants do."

"I'll see what I can do," the look in his eyes would have daunted a lesser person but Edna just laughed. She loved her son but found him rather tiresome and weak, especially after marrying that woman she didn't like.

"Just so you know, Gilbert, Barbara is now a member of this household and I'm changing her name from Foster to Coomb. I'll expect you to treat her like your child, Gilbert. She has no one in the world and I want her to be happy."

"Janice won't like this at all."

"The way it looks to me then, you have a choice to make. Besides, she'll be good company for Toby and he needs to know that he won't always be an only child. His mother mollycoddles him too much, and he's growing up into weakling, something that irks me very much."

"But we don't even know who she is."

"I know who she is and that's all that you need to know for now. I want you and your wife to treat this child well so she can forget the terrible life she's been subjected to for the past six months. Make sure you warn your loud-mouthed wife never to call her an orphan or say that she doesn't belong to this family. I've taken steps to obtain a new birth certificate for Barbara, and on it, you're indicated as her father and Janice as her mother."

"That's fraud, Mother."

"So, go ahead and report me to the Queen of England if you want. But remember, one word in the wrong ear and you'll lose everything. As I see it, I owe you and your wife no obligation. This house you live in and the money and good life you enjoy are because of my father, not yours. This is all Kildare wealth, nothing belonging to any Coomb. I rue the day I met that good-for-nothing, worthless man who was your father and decided to marry him. You've turned out to be no better than your father was, and now I must also take care of you and your wife and your son. Toby. at least, I love since he's such a precious little boy," her eyes were as cold as glaciers, and Gilbert swallowed nervously.

"I'll see what to do," he murmured grudgingly.

"And I expect you to do it all with a smile too," he gave her one which looked more like a grimace. "At least you're smiling. Now, go and tell your wife to prepare the room as I've told you and then make sure she and Toby are in the dining room. It's time Toby met his new sister, and Barbara her new family."

"Yes, Mother." The door closed softly behind him, leaving the woman chuckling under her breath.

"Come back here, you pesky little imp," the gentleman with the long hat and ivory cane shouted. Lawrence Trent, six years old, darted between people, slipping through their legs as they tried to catch him. He slipped into an alley and then ran as fast as his little legs could carry him. A door opened up ahead and a hand shot out and grabbed him, pulling him inside.

"Get in here, quick," an adult said, and he did so. "You did good, son," Peter Trent grinned at his son as he took the fat purse from his hands. "You'll be a great man one day."

"Peter, I don't like this at all," Salome his heavily pregnant wife spoke from the other corner of the room. "You've turned our son into a pickpocket and don't realize the danger you're putting him in. One day, someone will catch him and then he'll be lynched—or worse, shipped to the colonies as a slave. Is that what you want?"

"Woman, shut up," Peter roared, and Larry flinched as he went to sit beside his mother on the old but still strong couch. "You drop children like a rabbit and expect me to provide for you. Where do you think the sustenance is going to come from?"

"You could always go out and find work like all other decent men do."

"Would the few pennies paid out at the end of the week in the workhouses allow you to continue living in the luxury to which you're accustomed?"

"I would rather live under the bridge than feast on ill-gotten gains."

Peter opened the door, "Madam Perfect, the door is wide open, and you can go and live under the London Bridge. But mind that when you do, you're taking your brood with you."

Salome's response was to tighten her lips and turn her face to the wall. Her hands were playing with the shawl that she'd been crocheting before her son came running into the house.

Larry watched the harsh interchange with fear in his eyes. He loved his parents, but they were always quarrelling. It was because of his mother and four younger siblings that he had become a pickpocket. His father told him that it was the only way they could get food and keep the roof over their heads, and he believed him. The last thing he ever wanted was for his family to starve to death like many others he'd seen, or not have a decent home to live in, or to break up.

Their town house was in downtown London and had once belonged to a wealthy man who moved away when the area became unsafe for him to continue dwelling here. He had put the place up for rent and made Peter Trent his caretaker. The large house had been converted into four flats, and the Trents occupied one of the units on the ground floor. It had two bedrooms, a living room, and kitchen, as well as a veranda.

"Larry, come here," his father called out and he scrambled to his feet. "Tell your mother that if she wants to eat, then she should keep her big mouth shut," he glared at his wife. "Come, let's go to the market so I can buy you some foodstuffs to bring home."

"But Pa, those men who were chasing after me might still be out there and will see me."

"Go and change your clothes and put the black grease on your hair."

"Yes, Papa."

2

OUT OF THE SHADOWS

"**B**arb, don't be scared. I'm here to catch you," Toby Coomb crooned, looking up at the tree. "It's not a tall branch; jump down, and I'll catch you. Your brother is here to catch you," he said.

So intent on playing were the two children that they didn't hear the hissing sound made by Janice. She quickly faked a smile when she noticed her mother-in-law giving her "the look." The look made everyone in the household tremble, well, everyone except Barbara who was now seven years old. The little girl had perfected her grandmother's unnerving stare and her parents were on one occasion heard to remark that she would grow up into a terrifying woman. If not for her grandmother, she would have had her ears cuffed severely in an attempt to stop her from adopting any of her grandmother's characteristics.

"Toby has to go and lie down for his afternoon nap now," Janice said with a small laugh and Edna snorted. "Your brother needs his rest," she told Barbara, who merely shrugged and came sliding down the tree and into her brother's arms. The two children giggled together and for a moment ignored the adults who were seated on the front lawn of their house.

"Toby is four years older than Barbara, but I don't hear you mentioning that the child also needs a nap."

Janice ignored her mother-in-law's words and took her eleven-year-old son's hand. "Come along with me."

"But Mama," he protested and for his efforts, received a clipping in his ear.

Barbara stared at her mother's retreating back with puzzlement in her eyes. "Grandma, why do I get the feeling that my mother doesn't like me very much? Did I do something wrong?"

Edna laughed and pulled her close, "Barbara, you have a ludicrous imagination. Of course, your mother loves you."

"It feels like she doesn't like it when me and Toby play together."

"Your English is terrible, the correct way to say that sentence is, Toby and I, now repeat it correctly."

"Grandma, it feels like Mama doesn't like it when Toby and I play together."

"That's better, but you're wrong. He is a sickly child and needs much rest, unlike you who are so strong and beautiful," Edna said. "Also, you're too fast for him. I always tell you to slow down and not be so rough when playing with him, but you don't listen. You're a girl and should start behaving like one. If you want your mother to pay more attention to you then you need to start doing all the things she likes."

"Like what, Grandma?"

"For one, it wouldn't hurt for you to stop stealing the stable lad's clothes, putting them on and pretending to be a boy. That irks your mother, and she feels she's failing you as a parent."

"But I can't climb trees while wearing a dress, Grandma."

"That's another thing. Nice girls don't climb trees, wrestle with boys or swear like drunken sailors. You'll get hurt one day and it will break my heart."

"Grandma, I'm sorry," Barbara hung her head, waiting for the moment which wasn't long in coming.

'Oh, come here, you little imp," Edna could never stay angry at Barbara for long. "Now, get rid of that long face and let me see you smile." Barbara gave her grandmother a dazzling smile that lit up her whole face. "Oh Child," Edna sighed inwardly. "You'll break many hearts in your day."

"You spoil her too much, Mother," Gilbert walked onto the lawn. "Barbara, come here at once."

"Yes, Papa," she went and stood in front of him, swinging from side to side and her hands interlocked behind her back. Leaves were sticking out of her ruffled hair and the lace on her frock had ripped when she was climbing the tree, but she didn't care. She was happy that she had managed to climb the tree that had defeated her on so many occasions before.

"Go into your bedroom and get rid of those filthy clothes. Get cleaned up because it's nearly dinner time."

"Yes, Papa," Barbara obeyed more out of respect for her grandmother than her father. She always found him odd, especially when he gave her one of his funny looks, like he was about to say something to her but then thought better of it.

The servants called him "Mr. Hen," behind his back and she always wanted to ask what they meant by that but was afraid of having her ears boxed. Not that anyone would dare do that, at least not while her grandma was around.

Grandma! Just thinking about her sweet grandmother who smelled like roses and cinnamon had her grinning as she climbed the stairs. Her grandmother was afraid of nothing and no one, and would often tell her that fear was mostly in the mind.

"If a situation terrifies you, face it head on instead of running away to hide. Running away or hiding from it won't make it go away, it will be just delaying the inevitable."

"Why Grandma?"

"Because most times, the situation is more afraid of you than you are of it. When you run and hide, it gains more power over you. But when you stand and confront whatever it is that is making you scared, you become the master and subdue it."

She was smiling and counting the stairs, and as soon as she stepped onto the landing, ran into her mother.

"Wipe that foolish grin off your face," Janice said angrily.

"Yes, Mother," Barbara stood with her head lowered, eyes on the wooden tiled floor.

"Where are you going?"

"Papa told me to go and get cleaned up because it's nearly dinner time."

"Very well then, but don't make such a racket. Toby is sleeping."

"Mama, may I go and wake him up for dinner?"

"You'll do no such thing," Janice brought her face close to Barbara and she took a hasty step backwards. "Stay out of my son's bedroom, do you hear me?"

He was really scared and wanted his mother, but she was screaming in the other room. This always happened when she was getting another baby. The last three hadn't lived and Larry had watched as she sobbed over the small lifeless bodies. And as always, his father would disappear for days and only return when things were once more peaceful at home.

"Larry, why is Mama crying?" Adrian, his brother who was four years old asked him. "Is someone hurting Mama?"

"No." As the oldest, he had to be strong for his siblings for that's what Mama had told him to do. "Mama will be alright. We just need to wait for her to finish."

Sheyenne, his seven-year-old sister and immediate follower scrunched her face at him. "Finish doing what?"

He cleared his throat, feeling rather embarrassed. "Mama will be fine. Where are Lucy and Eugene?"

"Right here," Adrian said.

"I'll go check on Mama, but stay here," Larry got to his feet. He was hungry, and there was no food in the house. His father had said he was going to get them food, but Larry knew it would be days before he returned.

"We're hungry," Adrian whined.

"I know. Let me see if there's anything in the larder." His mother's piercing scream made him cringe, but he didn't want his siblings to see his fear. He was nearly ten and a big boy, and his mother depended on him to be strong for everyone.

"Hurry back."

"Yes, your majesty, Miss Sheyenne."

There was a little bit of oatmeal, which he mixed with water and carried back to the room. "I'll go out and get something more for us to eat, but just take this for now."

Within minutes, the four children had gobbled up the oatmeal but still looked hungry. He made a decision and walked to his mother's bedroom. The midwife was still attending to her as she screamed, and they didn't notice him slip out of the house. If only he could get a few pennies, he would be able to buy good food for his siblings. His mother would also need hot food after she had had the baby.

The life of a pickpocket was a dangerous one, and his father always warned him to be on the lookout and avoid people who were walking or standing in groups. A lone target was what he sought, and he knew that the only place he could find such was on the busy streets with people hurrying in all directions. Sometimes the pickings were easy and the people who he robbed didn't even feel his little hands as they slid their wallets out of their pockets. But sometimes, the intended targets were alert, probably because they'd been forewarned or else had been victims before. These were the hardest to rob because they were fast and brutal when they caught the pickpockets.

Even though Larry preferred to work alone, he knew of other small boys like him who were in the same trade, if one could call it that. Just last week, two of them had been caught and badly beaten up. One survived but the other died on his way to the hospital. He didn't intend to become a casualty, so he shook his head and turned to go back home.

"Watch where you're going, Son," a firm hand steadied him, and he looked up into the bluest eyes he'd ever seen. The man was even smiling at him. "You look lost, are your parents close by?"

Tears welled up in Larry's eyes as he saw the kindness in the man's eyes. People usually gave him glassy stares because of the way he was dressed, or else looked at him suspiciously. The man was well dressed, clearly a person of means, but he'd taken his time to stop and speak to him.

"Son, I won't hurt you, do you live around here?"

"Yes, Sir," he finally got his voice.

"How old are you?"

"Ten years old, Sir."

"You look small for your age," the man said and chuckled when Larry straightened out his shoulders and tried to look bigger than he actually was. "And you look very hungry. Would you like me to buy you some food?"

"My mother and sisters and brother are also hungry," Larry said. "I can't eat without them."

"You're a fine boy," the man said. "My name is Alistair Bramble and I was just on my way to visit one of my factories. If you come with me, I'll see to it that we go to the market and get some good food for you and your family."

"Yes, Sir," Larry felt like he could trust this man. His father had often told him of wealthy men who walked the streets of London looking for little boys they would kidnap and take away, never to be seen again. But Mr. Alistair looked like an honest man, someone who wouldn't hurt him.

Mr. Alistair soon finished his business and hailed a two-horse hackney and helped Larry up. "Careful now, Little Man,"

Alistair ruffled his hair. "We wouldn't want you to have an accident when your mother and siblings are waiting for you." And giving directions to the coachman, they were soon off. Larry's eyes widened when he saw the direction they were headed. "I just thought I should take you to my house so my housekeeper would get you some food to take back home."

The house turned out to be a large mansion in Hackney. Larry had once been around this area with his father and he'd always told himself that he would work hard and grow up to be as wealthy as most of Hackney's residents. But he didn't want to enter the house, recalling his father's words.

"You don't have to be afraid. Matilda, my housekeeper, will give you something to eat as you wait for her to pack what you need."

But he refused to enter the house and Mr. Alistair left him standing on the porch. He felt that he had annoyed the man, but he was afraid that if he saw the man's nice things, he might be tempted to steal them and get into trouble. His mother, whenever she could, always told him not to follow in his father's footsteps. So, he sat on the top step of the porch to see what would happen. The hackney driver was lounging against the vehicle, whistling tunelessly, and Larry got the feeling that the man had been here before.

Footsteps sounded on the wooden tiles, and the front door opened just as Larry turned. It was a middle-aged woman with a sweet smile. "Mr. Alistair told me that I would find you here," she said. "My name is Matilda, and Mr. Alistair is my older brother. I keep the house for him so you could call me the housekeeper," she threw her head back and laughed heartily at her own joke. Larry found himself liking this woman and he wondered if Mr. Alistair had any children. "I brought you some milk and pie, but my brother says you have refused to enter the house."

"I'm alright out here, Ma'am," he said politely.

"Very well then," she entered the house and returned carrying a small tray on which were two pieces of pie and a tall glass of milk. "Sit and eat because Mr. Alistair says he's soon leaving and will take you with him."

"Thank you, Ma'am."

~

Mr. Alistair turned out to be a widower who had lost his wife and two children ten years ago, to cholera and dysentery. He lived alone in the big house with his sister and a few servants.

"Your son looks like a fine man," he was telling Larry's mother, who seemed lost in her own world. She'd lost yet another baby at birth and didn't seem to notice the well-dressed man seated in her shabby living room. "I would like to take him as my pageboy and teach him what will help him in future."

Salome Trent nodded. "That would be nice."

"So, do I have your permission to take him to my house and bring him up like my own son? I promise that he will be visiting you once a week to bring you his wages and also some food."

"That would be nice," Salome repeated, and Mr. Alistair got the feeling that the woman wasn't paying much attention to whatever he was saying.

Larry was praying that his father wouldn't come in, for he would never let him go. This was the chance for him to stop being a pickpocket and get a good education. But he knew that his father would want him to continue with the "family business" as he called it.

"Take him away from here and keep him safe," Salome finally turned and looked at Mr. Alistair. "I worry about Larry because he's a very bright and intelligent boy, but if he continues to stay here, he'll soon get into a lot of trouble and I don't want to lose him."

"I will bring him on Saturday to see you," Mr. Alistair stood up and Salome did the same.

"Sir, please don't let my son ever return here. Keep him away from this place for the rest of his life, if need be."

3
FORGOTTEN MEMORIES

Someone or something was following her. It was really dark, and she was terrified, but her feet couldn't move, and she started screaming.

"Barbara, wake up," it took Edna nearly five minutes to finally calm the distraught child and wake her up.

"Grandma?"

"What's happening to you, Barbara?" Edna sat down on the child's bed. "You're ten and now a big girl who shouldn't be screaming her head off every night."

Barbara looked over her grandmother's shoulder to see whether either of her parents had come in to check on her, but like before, no one stood at the doorway.

"Your mother isn't feeling well," Edna noticed the disappointed look on the child's face. "But I'm here for you," she held out her hands and took the child in them.

"She never comes," Barbara said tearfully, "But if Toby even as much as sneezes, she fusses over him more than me and he's a big boy too."

"Barbara, that's enough. Stop with all the whining and self pity. You're a big girl and should understand that it isn't always about you." She kissed her on the forehead and laid her back on the pillow. "Now, go to sleep and let the rest of us get some shut-eye, too."

"Yes, Grandma."

Once her grandmother had left, Barbara turned to face the wall. At least the gas lamp was still on. She hated darkness, was terrified of the evils that lurked within it. Many times, she had asked her mother not to turn the lights off at night, but she would always tell her to behave like a big girl. She wondered why her own mother never once hugged or held her.

Whenever she was ill or frightened, it was always Grandma who was there for her. As for her father, he didn't bother much about her, and she'd learned not to expect much from him.

"Barbara?" Her brother's voice came to her from the doorway.

"Toby?" She quickly sat up and looked at her fourteen-year-old brother. Apart from her grandmother, he was the only one in this household who really cared, and she loved him deeply. "What are you doing out of bed?"

"Sh!" he held a finger to her lips. "I heard you crying but couldn't come in until Grandma had left."

"You shouldn't be here. If Mama finds you here, she'll be cross at both of us."

"Then we'll be silent," he sat on her bed and covered her up to her chin. "What made you cry?"

Barbara shrugged, "I guess I was having a bad dream."

"Granny says you have bad dreams because you're always reading adult books that you shouldn't even touch. Those books in Papa's study are not for us but you're always stealing one out of there to read."

Which was true; Edna had taught her how to read and write because she said Barbara was too intelligent for the half-brained governesses who taught Toby. The problem was that none of them stayed more than three months because her mother was a difficult woman. She criticized everything they did and picked quarrels with them so she could easily get rid of them.

Once Barbara had learned to read, she devoured any books she came across—including ones written in French, Spanish and even Latin. She read widely on all subjects, causing her grandmother to worry much.

Locking the room was a waste of time for she had learned how to climb up to the roof, get into the chimney, and slide down. She would often make a mess, which she cleaned up so she never got caught. She was also careful never to enter the study unless her father was travelling from home. She would then enter the study well prepared and spend hours closeted in the study, reading to her heart's content. Good thing was that her mother never bothered looking for her.

"Toby, books make a person clever and don't give you nightmares," she told her brother. "What's that in your pocket?"

"Oh," he ruffled her hair, "Mama brought some candy when she went to the village square. "Do you want some?"

Barbara nodded and her brother passed her a piece which she put in her mouth and immediately spat out. She made a face and wiped her tongue, "That tastes horrible," she made a gagging sound and Toby giggled. "Toby, never eat that again. It will make you ill."

"But I like candy."

"I know, and I'll get you some of the good ones from Grandma's bedroom. That," she pointed at the sticky substance in her brother's hand, "Isn't candy, it's poison."

When Larry turned thirteen, Matilda baked him a cake for his birthday. He'd been living with Mr. Alistair for three years now and was so happy. In those three years, the only time he'd seen his family was over Christmas when Mr. Alistair insisted on taking them a food basket.

His mother seemed to be shrinking with each passing year and much as he wanted to stay with her, living with Mr. Alistair was what kept his family fed. From the wages he earned as Mr. Alistair's pageboy, his mother was able to have money for food and clothes.

"You'll soon be a big boy and Mr. Alistair is thinking about sending you to Eton," Matilda told him one morning. "You're very intelligent and will make something of your life, Larry. Just be careful not to cross Mr. Alistair in any way."

"Yes, Ma'am."

Larry was a happy boy, but he had no idea that a storm was brewing and coming his way. For his father, who had been away from home for months, returned and demanded to see him. However, his mother wouldn't tell him where the boy was, no matter how much he beat her up.

But Peter Trent was a very shrewd man and managed to trace him to Alistair's home. Larry and his benefactor were seated on the front lawn enjoying mid-morning snacks when they became aware that someone was walking up the driveway.

"Larry, do you know who that person is?"

Larry looked up and his heart sank. It was his father, and that could only mean trouble. "That, Sir, is my father."

"Oh!" Alistair leaned forward in his seat and quietly observed the boy who looked terrified. "Did he hit you?"

"Sometimes," he said.

"Don't worry, I won't let him take you away from here."

They watched Peter as he came up to the house and then joined them at the lawn. "Good morning, Sir," he greeted Alistair politely.

"Good morning to you too, Larry tells me that you're his father."

"That I am, Sir."

"How is it that you've never been home whenever I visited your wife?"

"Sir, I'm a sailor, and my ship has been out in the Americas for nearly two years now. We just got back a few weeks ago but I was very ill and had to be placed under quarantine until I got better. When I arrived home yesterday, my wife told me that you had so graciously taken our son in."

"I'm very sorry about your situation. Is there anything I can do to help?"

Larry saw the greedy look enter his father's eyes and sighed inwardly. Mr. Alistair was such a good man that he always only saw the good in other people. He had clearly believed Peter when he told him he was a sailor, which was not true. According to what his mother had told him, his father had another wife and family and that was the reason he'd stopped coming home. The other woman was a widow with three children from her first marriage and she had the means. It was clear that Peter had gone to be with her because she lived in an affluent part of London and could give him all the money he wanted.

"Because of my illness, I'm not able to work and my family might starve," he bent over and coughed. "Sorry about that."

"Here, take my seat," Alistair stood up and let Peter sit down. "Let me ask my sister to prepare something for you to eat."

"You're most generous, Sir."

As soon as Alistair had disappeared out of sight, Peter turned to his son. "Son, you've landed yourself a big catch."

"Pa, Mr. Alistair is a very kind man and has been paying me a guinea a week to be his pageboy."

"So, you have money," Peter rubbed his hands together. "Your old man needs a loan. I promise to pay you."

"Pa, all that I earn is taken to Ma so she can take care of the house and the children."

"You must have something left over for your father," he insisted.

Larry shook his head, "I don't have any money."

"But a house such as this has many beautiful things. You need to pick one and bring it to me each time I come. I doubt that they will miss anything because they are wealthy," Peter said, and Larry's heart sank. "We can do good business, you and I, Son."

Alistair's return prevented Peter from saying anything more and he jumped back into the role he was playing of being a travel-weary sailor. Matilda brought him some milk and a piece of pie, and just as he finished eating it, he collapsed.

Alistair quickly sent for a doctor who came and pronounced Peter well enough, but the man pretended to be very weak.

"It's getting late, and you should spend the night here and leave in the morning," Alistair said, much to Larry's dismay. His father was up to something and it didn't bode well for anyone.

And the boy was right to be afraid, for that night, Peter left the guest room and went to the study. Mr. Alistair found him poking through his drawers and the two of them got into a terrible fight. Being the stronger, Peter soon subdued the man and left him for dead, robbing him of over two thousand pounds in cash along with some jewellery.

It was Matilda who found her brother bleeding on the floor of his study and called in the police. Things went downhill for the family from there. Matilda, really angry at Peter didn't once consider that Larry might be innocent.

"I warned my brother not to get too close to you and your family," she said coldly as the police arrested the thirteen-year-old boy who was weeping and took him away. "You and your whole family have defrauded my brother and taken advantage of his kindness. Make no mistake, I will have your father arrested and all of you will end up in prison until you pay for your crimes."

4

TORN AT EVERY EDGE

The first time Barbara witnessed a person coming into the world was when she turned twelve. Her birthday was coming up in a few days, and she wanted it to be very special. So, she sneaked down into the kitchen at a time when she knew it would be empty. Usually after lunch, Cookie and the other girls who helped her took a short nap, leaving the kitchen empty.

Cookie guarded her domain jealously and the only other person allowed to set foot in the kitchen was Grandma Edna. Even Janice stayed away from the highly temperamental cook who had no qualms about making her displeasure at her mistress known.

Barbara was slowly winning her over and she knew that Cookie wouldn't be too upset if she made her sweets, as long as she cleaned up properly afterward. And she usually also left a generous amount of the sweets for Cookie to take to her family.

She started putting the things she would need on the counter. There was a large pot boiling over the fire and the aroma of ham wafted through the kitchen. Barbara loved ham and she hoped that Cookie would come in and give her a piece before she left.

Then she heard something like a moan and then another. The sound was coming from beyond the kitchen, through the door that led to the servants' quarters. Barbara had never dared enter the forbidden area as her grandmother called it.

Apart from Cookie, the household had a scullery maid, a chambermaid, and Cookie's assistant, a girl not much older than she was and who had a big stomach. Anne was her name and Barbara often wondered if her own stomach would grow as big if she kept on eating. Her mother often told her that eating the wrong kind of food would make her stomach as big as Anne's. That puzzled the twelve-year-old very much because all manner of dishes were served at her father's table. So, which was the wrong kind of food?

When a louder moan reached her ears, curiosity got the better of her and she slipped through the door and entered the forbidden territory. She stood still, waiting to see if lightning would strike her or something, for she'd been made to promise her grandmother that she would never enter the servants' quarters.

But everything remained the same, well, apart from the moaning. Knowing that she could get into a lot of trouble if found here, she proceeded with a caution. The voices reached her and were coming from one of the rooms. The corridor was dark, and she pressed her frame against the wall just in case anyone had heard her and would come to check.

No one came, and she let out the breath she was holding. Feeling along the wall and walking slowly, she wondered why the servants didn't light up their corridor like it was in the rest of the house.

It never occurred to the girl that her mother didn't believe in indulging the servants and so didn't provide enough candles for their corridor too. But she could see a ray of light coming from one of the rooms and walked to the door which was slightly ajar.

"Don't cross your legs now," Cookie was saying in a harsh voice. "You should have crossed them before so we wouldn't be in this situation. Now that nincompoop has gone into hiding, leaving you to face all this trouble alone."

"It hurts so bad," Anne said in a weepy voice. "Make it stop."

"Well, next time you want to go and open your legs for that lout or any other good-for-nothing man, remember this pain and think twice about it."

"Mama, please make it stop," Anne wailed, and Barbara put a hand to her lips to prevent her gasp. Was Anne Cookie's daughter then?

"I'll slap you black and blue if you kill this child," Cookie roared. "Open those legs wide right now."

Barbara ventured to peep into the room and then almost at once, wished she hadn't. The sight was horrifying but she was also a curious girl and looked some more.

Megan, the scullery maid was standing over two pails that had steaming water in them.

"Megan, watch closely and see what I'm doing. Someday, you may be called upon to help a woman bring her child into the world and you need to be prepared."

"Yes, Ma'am."

"This is how babies are born. You make sure the head is coming out first or you can kill both mother and child."

"Mrs. Hunter," that was the first time Barbara heard the cook's name, "What if the legs come out first?"

"Then you make sure the mother stops pushing and then you try to push the legs back in gently and turn the baby."

"How?"

Cookie chuckled, "This one is coming out the right way so I can't show you what to do in case it is a breech birth as we call them. Megan, watch closely," the two women had no idea that the twelve-year-old was also watching very closely. "The head is almost out," Cookie was explaining about Anne's loud moans. "Stupid girl, stop shrieking like a banshee. I bet you weren't shrieking like this when you let that clod up your skirts. Keep quiet or I'll slap you so hard I'll give you more reason to cry."

"Mrs. Hunter, it's coming," Megan sounded excited.

"Anne, take a deep breath, bear down and push as hard as you can."

Barbara nearly fell into the room, eyes as round as saucers. She heard a squishing sound and then saw a dark thing pop out from between Anne's legs. "It's a boy," Cookie cried out with joy and she received the child." At least, I won't have to worry about this one getting pregnant in fourteen years' time," she said.

"Mrs. Hunter, what do I do with this thick rope? Should I pull it out?"

"No, never do that because you could kill the mother. It's the cord that connects mother and child but now that this baby is born, it has no more use. What you do is measure half a span on the baby's side then tie with a piece of string and cut," she demonstrated, and Barbara took note. "As a midwife, you must always have a sharp knife to use. Dip this in hot water before because we don't want any dirt around the baby."

"I still see more rope."

"Yes, that part is left inside the mother and has to come out. Once the baby is born and you have securely tied and cut the cord, hand the child to the mother to begin nursing right away. It will help the rest of this rope as you call it, to come out. Gently rub over the stomach like this," and another squishing sound produced a thick mass. "This is the placenta and you bury it or throw it into the outhouse."

The Debtors' Prison in Fleet Street was a horrible place and Larry watched his family wasting away. His father had been arrested and tried for attempted murder but for some reason, he was sent to Fleet Prison instead of Newgate. And because Matilda claimed that he owed her brother nearly three thousand pounds, the prison term was indefinite.

"Until such a time as you will fully settle the debt you owe Mr. Alistair Bramble, together with all interest accrued," the magistrate had pronounced.

Because of the widely publicized incident, Peter's landlord threw them out of the house, and with nowhere else to go, they all ended up in Fleet Street with him. Larry refused to speak to his father, who had come and ruined their lives.

Their family cell was a small room that had lice and rats, and with nothing, they did the best they could. Since he wasn't the prisoner, he was allowed to come in and go and he tried his best to bring his family food. But times were hard, and finding honest work for a fifteen-year-old boy was hard. But he'd made a promise to his mother that he would never return to a life of crime again, no matter what happened.

"Mama, I'm so sorry," he told her as she lay languishing in the prison. "I should never have let Papa stay at Mr. Alistair's house." He missed the kind man who had seemed to be their way out of poverty but who had nearly paid for his generous and charitable deeds with his life. Larry had sat in the courthouse when his father was being tried, and as the plaintiff, Mr. Alistair and Matilda were also present. But they didn't as much as spare him a glance and his heart broke. They had trusted him and because of his father, that trust had ended.

Salome simply touched her son's face. "If I die, please take care of your siblings. You'll be free one day, promise me that you'll get as far away from your father as possible."

"I promise you, Ma."

5
THE DARK SIDE

In years to come, Barbara would always thank her brother for the end of her dream world as she called her years of innocence. Toby wanted a book from their father's study but as usual, the room was locked. She was sure that if he had asked their mother, she would have opened the door for him. But as it is, he wanted the book right away and their mother was nowhere to be found.

"What will you give me if I get the book for you?" Barbara asked cheekily, a twinkle in her eyes.

The two children were in their grandmother's bedchamber which was the only place they could be together without fearing that Janice would burst in and drag Toby away. Even though he had turned seventeen, their mother still treated Toby as if he were five years old.

Grandma Edna was sleeping, yet it was only mid morning, which struck Barbara as very odd. Her grandmother always said that only the sick, little babies, and the elderly slept during the day, and especially mid morning.

"I'll give you the money Mama keeps in a jar in her bedroom," Toby said.

"Go and bring it first, and then I'll get you the book. Make sure no one sees you, and no slamming of doors, Grandma is sleeping."

"Okay," Toby whispered loudly as he left the room.

"What are the two of you now scheming, Barbara," her grandmother's drowsy voice startled her. "I could hear you and Toby whispering to each other and that's never a good sign."

"Grandma," Barbara rose from the floor and brushed her dress with her hands. "You told me that only old people, babies, and the sick sleep during the day. And you're not old or a baby." She drew closer to the bed and looked down at her grandmother. "Grandma, are you ill?"

Enda gave a tinkling laugh while shaking her head, but Barbara noticed that she avoided looking at her. When she opened her mouth to say something, the door opened, and Toby walked into the room.

"Barbara, I got it," Both fists were clenched tight. "Oh Grandma," he came to a sudden halt as soon as he realized they were not alone, putting both hands behind his back.

"What's that in your hands, Toby?" Edna gave him "the look" and he was soon spilling his guts out, much to Barbara's disgust. Why couldn't people see that beneath all that sternness on Grandma Edna's face was a very soft and gentle person? Now she wasn't going to be able to snoop into her father's study. But Edna surprised both children.

"So, you want to sneak into your father's study? Why don't you go ahead and do it then while Toby and I stand as your lookout people?"

"Really Grandma?" Barbara was excited. She would be turning fourteen soon and wanted to find out if this year, her parents had finally bought her a gift for her birthday. And also, to get the book her brother wanted. "But Grandma, Papa's study is locked," she was hoping that her grandmother had the keys to the study so she wouldn't have to slither down the chimney. On her last excursion down, she'd noticed that she had to wiggle a lot to make it down. It was like the chimney had grown smaller.

"I know that you like to sneak down through the chimney, though you're growing too big to continue doing so without getting hurt," Edna winked at her. "Go ahead, I think you find it to be more fun that way."

With a broad grin on her face, Barbara made her way outside the house, knowing that her grandmother would keep her word. If there was anyone she trusted in this whole world, it was her grandmother, and she knew that for as long as Grandma was around, she would always be safe.

Autumn was in the air, and much as she liked listening to the wind blowing and watching the trees shedding their leaves, she preferred to be safely ensconced in the warm house. Also, as usually happened when autumn finally descended on them, her father liked lighting a fire in the hearth in his study, so this would probably be her last excursion down the chimney for this year, or maybe forever. The heat and smoke always prevented her from embarking on her daring feats. And come next year, she might not fit into the chimney. She knew that she had grown, for her grandmother made her wear heavier undergarments.

"So the men won't be looking at you too much," Grandma had said when Barbara protested that too much clothing made her uncomfortable. *"As a growing woman, you need to keep yourself properly covered because that will ensure that you stay safe. Do not*

lead others into temptation, Child." And Barbara had started wearing the thicker undergarments, just to please her grandmother, while wondering what leading others into temptation meant.

She had a little bit of a struggle going down even though the chimney was clean. Their usual chimney sweep had been by just last week to clean it up in preparation for the autumn fires. But Barbara was smiling as she stealthily climbed down, listening for any signs of a warning from Toby or her grandmother as they had agreed. When she had just a few more feet to descend, she froze. There were people inside the study and the voices clearly didn't belong to Grandma Edna or Toby. It was her parents and she heard them mention her name.

"Mother is very ill, and all we have to do is wait for a few weeks more. Then all should go according to plan. Let's not agitate her because she adores Barbara, and that can create trouble for us," her father was saying.

"We have to be very careful not to antagonize the old battleaxe," her mother agreed. "But what will we do with Barbara?"

"Like I said, in just a few weeks' time, our plans will be complete. Make sure that Barbara and Toby don't find out that Mother is very sick. Those two are as thick as thieves, and who knows what they might decide to do?"

"No matter what I do, Toby just won't listen to me, especially when it comes to Barbara. It's like she's bewitched him and your mother. That girl has them both eating out of her hands, and nothing I do makes any sense and your mother encourages it."

❦

It was his mother's cry which woke him up, and Larry quickly sat up in the dark cell. "What is it, Ma?"

"Larry, I don't think I'll see morning," she said breathlessly, for she could barely get the words out of her mouth. "I can feel death coming for me."

"Ma, please don't say that. I wrote to Mr. Alistair after Papa died, and I know he will release us. Please Ma, hold on and don't leave me."

Salome shook her head, but her son couldn't see her in the darkness. She knew she was dying, and besides, she was tired of living. What was there to live for anyway? Six wasted years of her life behind bars and all because of her husband who was a greedy and wicked man. One by one, she'd watched her four children die in prison and had no idea if they even got a decent burial. Larry told her they did, but he was a good boy who would say anything just to make her happy.

And then her husband had finally followed, but for him, she hadn't mourned. He was the reason why their lives were such a mess. Larry had tried to get them out of their poverty and miserable lives, but Peter had to go and mess things up.

"Larry, come closer," she said, holding out a hand in the darkness. She heard her son, her only remaining child crawling on the floor and then he was by her side. "You're a good boy and have been punished for the sins of your parents. Forgive me, Larry."

"Ma, there's nothing to forgive," he felt around and took her hand in his. "Ma, this isn't the time to give up. The end is in sight, and we shall be free."

"You don't know that."

"I know Mr. Alistair and he's a good man. I just have the feeling that he will pardon us from Papa's debt, and we will be freed."

"Larry, promise me one thing."

"What is it, Ma?"

"That you will never put your hand out to commit a crime, no matter how hungry or poor you are."

"I promise you, Ma."

"Live a life devoid of crime."

"I promise you, Ma."

"And when the time comes, only marry a queen."

"Ma?"

She chuckled softly, her voice getting weaker. "The queen of your heart," she said. "Don't go after a woman because she has money or means. Your father paid for his sins so many times, but he just wouldn't learn."

Larry didn't want to talk about the man who had messed up their lives. If only his father had died many years before, he thought.

"Forgive," his mother was saying. "I know you carry a big grudge against your father for what he did. But Son, forgive him." Larry was silent. He didn't think he had it in him to forgive that wicked man. "The Lord blesses those who honour their parents, no matter how wicked or bad they were."

"But Ma . . ."

"Larry, don't break my heart again."

"Ma!"

"I want to go knowing that your heart is clean, Larry. Leave vengeance for the Lord." Larry wanted to laugh out loud. His father was dead so what would vengeance from the Lord do?

"Peter will have to answer to the Lord for his crimes, don't let bitterness and anger against him hold you in prison. This is a physical prison and you'll one day walk out of here, but the prison of the soul is the worst. Even if you excel in life but still have bitterness and unforgiveness, you'll be in prison. Get out of it now, my Son."

"Ma," he said at last, "I'll try."

"That's all I ask, and may God be with you till we meet again."

And those were the last words that she said for she slipped away while he was still holding her hand.

6
STEEL HEARTS

"**Y**ou're a big girl now, and I don't want you to cry," Edna was trying to be strong for the child. She knew that she only had a few weeks left to live and didn't want this beloved child to suffer at the hands of her daughter-in-law and henpecked son. Janice controlled Gilbert who might otherwise have been a good person. As soon as she had seen her doctor and he told her the bad news, she had searched for a convent that took in teenage girls and taught them more than just housekeeping, sewing, and knitting. Sister Mary Claire of St. Agatha's Convent and School for Enlightened Girls had promised her that arithmetic, history, and religion were also part of the school's curriculum.

On the pretext of visiting an old friend, Edna had paid a visit to the school where her little lamb would be for about four years and was satisfied with what she saw. It was a very good institution, and Barbara would be happy there.

Edna knew that with her gone Barbara's days in this household were numbered. But she had made special arrangements and hoped that Mr. Forbes, her solicitor would do the right thing when the time came. Barbara's stay at the convent would be taken care of, and she would be placed in one of the upper dormitories for the children of those who could pay. There were also orphans taken care of by the convent, and these didn't enjoy the same privileges as the others. Her Barbara would be comfortable at the school, and once she turned eighteen, Mr. Forbes had instructions to give her five thousand pounds so she could open up the candy store she dreamed about. Yes, Edna could go in peace knowing that Barbara would never have to suffer.

"Grandma, but I don't want to go," Barbara clung to her grandmother, weeping brokenly. "I'll be a good girl, I promise. And I will learn how to sew and knit to make Mama happy, and I won't make noise, so Papa won't be cross. I promise, Grandma."

"You're breaking my heart, Child," Edna's voice broke. "School is good for you for it will turn you into an independent woman. In about two decades, we'll be coming to the end of this century and a lot is happening in England and the world too, making opportunities for women. You need a good education to be the kind of woman I want you to be in future. Or do you just want to find a husband, get married, and start having many babies?"

"No, Grandma, but I can learn everything from Toby's governesses, and I promise to listen to them. And I don't understand why you haven't found a school for Toby the way you did for me. He's older than me, how is it that he's not going away?"

"Barbara, I've always told you that comparing yourself to others is for people with mediocre minds. You're a very intelligent young woman who has made me proud and I want you to remember that only the strong conquer the world."

"Please, Grandma," Barbara begged.

"Enough of the whining," Edna's tone was stern, something Barbara had never heard before. Her grandmother had never addressed her with anything but a soft and gentle voice. "It's time for you to see the world and this is the only way."

"Will you come and visit me in school?" She finally resigned herself to the fact that all the begging and pleading in the world wouldn't get her anywhere.

"But of course, my love," Edna hugged her and something in her voice made Barbara feel that she was only saying those words to calm her down.

"Will I be able to come home and see you and Toby?"

"Sister Mary Claire says students get to go home once a year, which is over the Christmas holidays. You'll be able to come and see us then."

"But I wish I didn't have to go away," she said in a small voice.

But much as she pleaded, her fate was sealed, and on a cold Monday morning, her clothes were packed into two suitcases, which were then placed on top of her father's carriage and she bid farewell to the beloved woman who had always loved her even when her parents didn't have time for her. Toby was crying openly as he waved, running after the carriage until it drove out of the estate. His last words to her were, "Barbara, I promise I'll write to you," he said, ignoring his mother's angry glance. "And I'll come and see you and bring you home for Christmas."

She smiled sadly, waving back at her brother who had grown up so much. He was a very handsome young man, and at eighteen, he was already turning many girls' heads. She liked going to the village square with him because she got to see the ladies swooning over her dashing brother.

And Tanya, the girl who worked in the village grocery often gave her a lot of free candy while she flirted with Toby.

"Farewell, my beloved Toby," she called out, leaning out of the window and waving back at him. "Wait," she screeched, and the coachman stopped the carriage, sending her father flying to the other side. Barbara scrambled out of the carriage and ran down the driveway, Toby in hot pursuit. "Grandma," she flung herself into Edna's arms, "I'll miss you so much. I wish I didn't have to go."

Edna hugged the girl for a long while and then with a deep sigh, released her. Toby also hugged her and the two of them walked her back up the driveway to the carriage, each holding one of her hands. Once they got there, there was another bout of weeping.

"Enough now," Edna said in a firm voice. "Come," she helped Barbara up into the carriage. "Be a good girl for the nuns and do me proud, okay?"

Barbara nodded, tears pouring down her cheeks. "Yes, Grandma. Will I see you at Christmas?" Which was another nine months away because she was joining the school in early spring.

"Shall we wait until that time comes before we make any promises?"

"Yes, Grandma."

The drive that took two days was done mostly in silence. As the carriage left her home town of Bletchley and headed north, Barbara felt fear within her heart. She had a funny feeling within that all was not right. Nothing had been right from that day months ago when she'd over heard her parents talking about how sick her grandmother was. But Grandma

43

Edna had continued to brush off Barbara's questions about her health.

"Your new school is in Wolverton," her father told her. "That's not too far from home and we shall visit you," he said, but she didn't believe him, not for a single moment. There was something in his smile and eyes that made her feel that she was dealing with a stranger, not her father. "But you have to promise to be a good girl and not try to run away. The school is surrounded by woods, and wild animals dwell there, so you would be torn to pieces . . ."

"Stop," she shouted, covering her ears with her hands. "I don't want to listen to you," she started crying and moved farther away from him, pressing her face against the wall of the carriage. It was as though her father derived pleasure in frightening her, and she decided that for the rest of the journey, she would just ignore him.

After the conversation she'd overheard between him and her mother, she'd started watching her grandmother to see if there were any signs of illness and she found plenty. The once robust skin was turning translucent and it seemed like her veins started sticking out. Then the moments when Grandma would suddenly doze off in her chair, something she never used to do, and also the fact that her food was nearly always uneaten. She refused to dine in the large dining hall, and Barbara or one of the maids would bring her food to her bedchamber, only to carry the tray away with barely anything touched.

Why hadn't she insisted on her grandmother telling her the truth? What was going to happen to her now?

"Don't look so glum," her father tried again. "Christmas isn't that far away, and I'll come and bring you home. Your grandmother and Toby will be waiting. I bet you can't wait to see them again."

Barbara merely shrugged and continued staring out of the window. At the five or so inns where they stopped to change horses and rest, she was shown into a parlour where for the most part she was alone. The temptation to slip out of the inns and run away was so great, but she had nowhere to go. If she returned home, her grandmother would be angry with her and that was something she didn't want.

On the third day, they entered the town of Wolverton. "We'll soon be there," her father said. But like before, she ignored all his comments and concentrated on seeing as much of the new town as possible. Who knows, she might one day get the chance to leave and she wanted to be as prepared as could be.

Wolverton was a railway town and for a moment, Barbara forgot her sadness and watched with sparkling eyes as they passed by the station. People were coming and going, and she could see large locomotives in the yard. If her parents thought she would stay in school for that long and not come home, they were mistaken. She would save her pocket money and then take a train back home.

But her hopes were soon dashed when the carriage left the town and started down a long and winding road which took them many miles from the town centre. There were tall trees all around them and she recalled her father's words. This was indeed a thick forest and she was scared that a wild animal might emerge from the bush and attack them. Nothing of the sort happened, however, and after driving for nearly five hours from the town, she saw the large imposing gates ahead.

"That is St. Agatha's Convent," her father said unnecessarily, and she nearly rolled her eyes. She could see that this road led right up to the gate, which was surrounded by a tall natural fence. As they drove in, she noticed that the fence was so thick it would be impossible for anyone to sneak through it. It was nearly another two miles before she saw the large buildings in the distance. It looked like it was a castle of some kind and she felt her heart pumping with excitement. Many places to hide, oh what an adventure, she thought. She and Toby had often imagined themselves to be knights who lived in a castle. She couldn't wait to get there and explore, and then she would have many stories to tell Toby when she went back home for Christmas.

As the carriage drew closer to the castle, she could barely sit still and felt like a princess coming to her palace, the kind that Grandma had told her stories about.

"Oh Papa," she forgot her anger towards him, "I like my new school," she clapped her hands and stuck her head out of the window for a better view. "It looks so big."

Gilbert Coomb felt a pang in his heart that he couldn't describe, but he quickly quashed it. He didn't want Barbara to see any vulnerability or signs of weakness in him. This child was intelligent beyond her years and now wasn't the time to show any kind of weakness.

"I'm glad you like your new school," he told her as the coachman drew up to the steps that seemed to go on forever upwards. "Come, Gus will bring you trunks in. Let's go and meet Sister Mary Claire."

The two tall doors opened and four women dressed in nuns' garb stood there. As she climbed the steps slightly behind her father, Barbara paused to take a look back and gasped. She could see over the huge fence for miles but there were only trees. It was like their canopy made a carpet that looked deceivingly safe and inviting. Wild animals inhabited those woods and she shuddered slightly, resuming her climb.

"Welcome to St. Agatha's Convent and School for Enlightened Girls," a formidable looking woman with a permanent frown on her brow tried to smile and reminded her of a picture of a grinning wolf she'd seen. She hid a giggle behind a discreet cough. "Come this way at once."

Getting registered in her new school didn't take long, and after some money exchanged hands, she was allowed to walk her father only as far as the large wooden doors. She wasn't even allowed to step out and see him to the carriage.

"Be a good girl now," were his last words before he stepped out and the doors were shut. Hearing the metal bolts hitting home felt so final, and she stood there staring at the closed doors for a long while. Suddenly, she was really frightened. Something wasn't right; she could feel it. A loud gong sounded, nearly making her jump out of her skin.

The world had forgotten all about him and he was sure he would die behind bars like the rest of his family had. With his father gone and the debt unpaid, he was no longer allowed to come and go as he pleased.

Mr. Alistair had ignored his pleas and decided he would pay for his father's sins. Well, he was alone and to fend for himself, he offered to run errands within the prison for the guards and even though they didn't pay him with money, he was at least able to get one good meal a day. And also, he had to vacate his cell to give room to a family of five who were also there for the same reason that his had been. Only in the case of the Smiths, a travelling salesman had delivered a wooden stove to the house even though they didn't want it, and when they couldn't pay up, he had them thrown into prison.

Larry felt sorry for them and whenever he would get some food, he would bring part of it to the family.

"The Lord will bless you and remember you," Mrs. Smith would always tell him. The man was surly, and Larry learned to steer clear of him.

PART II
THE MINING ERA

7

A LIVING ABYSS

St. Agatha's Convent and School for Enlightened Girls wasn't what Barbara had envisioned it to be. The only beautiful part of the school was the castle, which had four large classrooms and four beautiful dormitories as well as the convent itself. The rest of it was something else.

There were two dormitories for poor students who were orphans, and these were nothing more than sheds built out of timber and not properly reinforced so that during the rainy season, water seeped in through the gaping holes. But these were built far from the castle itself and there was a thick fence separating the two areas; this was because of the benefactors who visited the school. They were made to believe that only the castle provided lodgings for the girls.

They would be shown the two beautiful dormitories as well as the classrooms, the dining hall, kitchen, infirmary, and the washing area. If any asked to see the rest of the school, they were gently but firmly informed that the castle was the school and beyond that was the farm where animals and grains were stored for feeding the girls. Also, the poorer students who didn't have good clothes were kept hidden even though it was because of them that the school got any donations.

Barbara hated the lies that she soon realized were part of this community, and she bid her time until she could run away. Her first two months in St. Agatha's were pleasant enough because she was placed in one of the four beautiful dormitories that were subdivided into cubicles housing four girls each. But in the third month, she was called out of class by the Mother Superior and told to go and collect all her belongings.

"Am I going home?" She was excited but this faded when the woman gave her a look that frightened her. It was like Sister Mary Claire really hated her and went out of her way to humiliate her.

"Don't be an imbecile," she was told, "Follow Sister Caritas, who will show you where you belong." And the woman walked away, leaving her standing in the middle of the courtyard wondering what to do.

"What's wrong?" A girl of about her age came up behind, startling her. "What did that horrible woman want?"

"She directed me to take my trunks and follow Sister Caritas to where I belong," Barbara said, noticing the other nun who seemed to be cowering in the doorway. "Let me go and find out what's going on."

"I'll come with you. My name is Nancy Burton and I've been here for a year. This is my second year and I can't wait to turn eighteen and get away from this place for good."

"I'm Barbara Coomb and just came in two months ago."

"I've noticed you sitting all alone. Don't you want to make any friends?"

Barbara shrugged, "With time, I guess." They stood before the petite nun. "Mother Superior says you're to show me where I belong."

"Get your trunks and come down here quickly."

Nancy helped her get her trunks and they followed the nun out of the castle, into the courtyard, crossed it and then to the gate that separated the castle from the barns as the students referred to this part of the school.

Barbara stopped, suddenly realizing what was happening. "Sister Caritas, I think there's been a mistake."

The nun shook her head, "Your parents won't pay any more money for your maintenance and this is where you now belong. You'll take your classes on this side of the school, too, from now on, so I hope you brought all your belongings. No one from this side is allowed to cross this gate or you'll be in serious trouble."

"I'll find out what is going on," Nancy promised when she had helped her new friend into the dormitory. These were two large adjoining halls which were more like old barns, probably used to stable the Lord of the Castle's horses in medieval times, Barbara thought.

Instead of cubicles, old curtains separated the girls' beds. At least the others were out in class and no one was there to witness her fall from grace.

"Don't worry," she told Nancy, "I'll be alright."

"I'll be coming to see you every day," Nancy promised, but Barbara merely turned away. Like everyone else in her life, this one was also just giving her false promises. She had written nearly five letters to her grandmother and Toby but had not received a single response. Maybe they had already forgotten her, but she refused to believe that Grandma Edna who loved her so much could have just abandoned her.

The classrooms for the poor students turned out to be no better than their dorms. Their desks were broken down and most of the time they had to teach themselves whatever lessons were due since the nuns didn't bother much with them.

"Oh, Grandma," Barbara wept each night as she listened to the rats scurrying around the dorm in search of something to eat, "why have you abandoned me?"

Barbara peered through the gap between the curtains of her cubicle to see if any of the other girls were still awake. Their soft snores told her that she was the only one awake at that dark hour of the night.

Late nights were the only times she felt alive. Everyone was asleep—even the rats and bats that were permanent residents of this old and ugly building. The nun in charge had a walled cubicle right at the door, probably to ensure that none of the girls got out. But Barbara had found another way out of the barn and she used it every day to go and meet with Nancy.

The girl had kept her promise from the first day they met and became her best friend even though their lives were worlds apart. Her current life was a far cry from what it had been when she first got here. St. Agatha's Convent and School for Enlightened Young Woman promised to turn the girls into prospective housewives, the kind that gazed adoringly at their husbands, produced a brood of children and kept good homes. That was the side that catered to the children of the entitled, like Nancy. The other side was totally different, however. Here on this side, all they were taught was how to milk, till the ground, churn butter, bake, and other hard menial jobs. They weren't expected to ever find good husbands because they were poor and even if they did, would end up as servants of their colleagues on the other side of the wall.

Barbara was sick of this place and couldn't wait to get out. She had turned sixteen and waited for a gift from her grandmother with much anticipation even though the woman had not written her, not once. But none came, not even a card and she began to wonder if she had imagined all the loving kindness the older lady had given her.

In the two years that she'd been in this place, she had quickly learned that being chirpy only made a person easily singled out for punishment by the dour nuns. The convent had about twenty nuns, but only ten of them were actively involved with the school. They never smiled or showed any kindness, and Barbara sighed in the darkness, creeping back to bed. She hoped Nancy wouldn't wait for her for too long and get caught. It was too cold to go out and she'd changed her mind.

She sat on her bed and hugged her knees, letting the tears flow freely. Her knees were hard from constant kneeling to scrub the floors with a hard brush and lye. According to the Mother Superior, Barbara was the worst child she had ever had to take care of in her forty years as a nun.

"You're rude and cheeky. Trying to teach you anything is a waste of time because you're no better than the village idiots who roam the countryside with drool all over their faces." That was in her third month after she had been moved from the castle to the barn.

"Good, then expel me and send me back home," Barbara had retorted, looking for the chance to have the woman kick her out so she could go back home to her beloved grandmother and brother.

Instead of that, she earned herself a slap that sent her flying across the room.

"I'll not have your insolence infecting other children. And for your loose mouth, you've just earned yourself a whole week in solitary."

And solitary had been hell. For her penance, she received two lashes across her back every single day and had to recite prayers for hours asking forgiveness for her horrible sins. Fed only a plate of lumpy oatmeal once a day, Barbara had wept every day and called out to her grandmother to come and get her. But her prayers went unanswered. At the end of seven days' punishment, a new girl emerged. Quiet but seething within, she learned to blank her face so that no one ever knew what she was thinking. She didn't want anyone ever hitting her again or sending her into solitary confinement.

Then she was brought out to the courtyard where all the girls had assembled to witness her humiliation. She stank and wasn't allowed to clean up, but the Mother Superior wanted to make an example of her. After letting the other girls jeer, she directed her to go and wash off at the pond down the hill because she didn't deserve to use the bathrooms with the other girls.

"Don't worry," Nancy had followed her, much to her surprise. "Everyone is mean to you because they're afraid of you. No one survives solitary."

"What?"

Nancy nodded, "The last two girls who were placed in solitary confinement were carried out dead after seven days. You're going to be something of a legend, but please don't do anything that will send you back in there."

"I'll run away and never come back to this horrible place," Barbara said. "I hate this place."

Nancy only laughed, "How will you run away? There's nowhere to go and the forest is really thick. If the animals don't get you, then the mad men who live in there will find you and do abominable things to you. Last year, two girls tried to run away but their bodies were found badly mutilated. Just keep your head down and don't attract anyone's attention."

"I don't care if anyone kills me along the way," Barbara said, stripping and tossing aside her filthy garments. She held the foul-smelling piece of soap that had been tossed to her by Sister Caritas.

"Throw that horrible-smelling soap into the river," Nancy told her, pulling out a sweet-smelling cake from her pocket. "Use this instead."

"Are we allowed to have such?" The soap smelled of roses, reminding her of her grandmother and tears filled her eyes.

"Did the soap get in your eyes?"

"No," Barbara wept, lathering herself lavishly for she had no idea when she would be able to use such sweet-smelling soap again. She jumped into the freezing pond and thought her heart had stopped.

"You need to move around, or you'll freeze to death."

"Good! Then my parents can come and carry my lifeless body out of this place," and she closed her eyes. It was a pity the pond wasn't very deep, for the water only reached her waist. Much as she tried to get herself to sink, she found herself standing in the pond. She turned her back on Nancy and ignored the sounds of nature around her. Misery covered her like a thick blanket, and she began to pray for death.

A big splash startled her, and her eyes flew open, "What was that?"

"Quick, get out at once. Sometimes snakes also come to the pond. You don't want to be bitten now, do you?"

Barbara needed no second bidding but scrambled out and stood trembling on the bank as Nancy threw a coarse towel around her. "Thank you." Her teeth were chattering, and she felt really cold.

"Get dressed and let's go back to your dormitory. I'll bring you some hot chocolate."

"How?"

"Sister Caritas will bring it to you. I've been slipping her a guinea or two so she can make sure you're alright."

"Won't you get into trouble hanging around with me?" Barbara was genuinely puzzled as to why this pretty and wealthy girl should want to be her friend. "Everyone else is treating me like a leper. Why are you here?"

Nancy shrugged, "I don't care about other people. Besides, I'm doing nothing wrong."

"Well, when my grandmother comes to visit me soon, I'll let her know how kind you've been to me."

"I look forward to meeting her," Nancy smiled. "She sounds like a wonderful person."

"She is, and so is my brother. I know they will both come to see me, and I'd like for you to meet Toby. He's so handsome. Who knows, you might fall in love, and then you'll be my sister."

"Barbara, stop saying that." Nancy's face turned bright red.

"Toby will really like you."

"Shall we not speak of that? If anyone hears us, we'll have to do penance for thinking immoral thoughts," Nancy said. They soon got to the dormitory and Nancy stopped at the door. "Go in and I'll get Sister Caritas to bring you some hot chocolate."

"Thank you."

"And when we go home for the holidays, I'd like for you to come to my home in Leighton to visit. We'll have so much fun."

Barbara shook her head, "Thank you for the kind offer, but I don't think I can. You see, my brother and grandmother will want to hear all about my experience at school, and I don't think there'll be time to visit. But you're a good friend for thinking about me."

But no one visited her, not for two years, nor was she allowed to go home for the first Christmas. The second was coming up and the other students were so excited to be going home to see their families. Would anyone come for her this Christmas? She bowed her head and prayed. She really had to get out of this place before she ran mad.

8

ONE BIG MESS

"I should be in Rome with the Pope for Christmas," Sister Mary Claire hissed at the twenty girls who cowered before her. "Yet I'm forced to be here with you," she glared at Barbara especially. "You're nothing but a lot of misfits whose families have no desire to have them back home for the holidays. Let's get one thing clear, there's no money left to enable the school to hire any temporary staff to cook for you, so I expect you to take care of yourselves. The regular staff have all gone for Christmas and will be back in the New Year." She turned to Barbara, "You're the oldest and I expect you to be in charge of the rest. You're also in charge of the kitchen and cleaning up. Is that understood?"

"Yes, Mother Superior," Barbara said. She was resigned to the fact that once again, she wouldn't be going home. Nancy had told her parents to ask Mother Superior to let Barbara go home with them when no one came for her on closing day, but the nun refused. She told the Burtons that Barbara's family would be coming in two days' time to take her home. For two days, Barbara had waited and watched but it was now clear that all that had been a lie. Maybe her grandmother was still angry at her for her many tricks, but she'd written to tell her that in the two years in school, she'd become older and wiser.

"Good," Mother Superior said, "Now go to the pantry and find out what is there for you to prepare for dinner. And know this; that food has to last you until the New Year when the rest return and we can restock the pantry."

After glaring at her charges one final time, the angry nun turned and walked down the corridor toward her private quarters. Only a handful of girls, Nancy being one of them, were privy to the nuns' private quarters, given their privileged statuses.

To Barbara, St. Agatha was the epitome of pretentiousness and hypocrisy. It catered for girls from wealthy families who paid much to be there while also claiming to take care of the poor who were neglected, like Barbara. She wondered why they were forced to pray to a God who was clearly prejudiced against those who were poor. Her grandmother had taught her that God loved the poor and Jesus took care of them in His day. Yet out here, she and her fellow students were treated differently from the others. What was worse, they were forced to endure the scorn of the other entitled girls.

One such girl had nearly had herself choked to death when she called Barbara a delinquent whose parents thought she was too much trouble and wanted nothing to do with her. Wasn't that the reason they never once visited her, nor allowed her to go home? Nancy had broken up the fight and bribed the girl with a jar of sweets, and they hushed up the matter, else Barbara would have been in a lot of trouble.

The pantry yielded half a sack of dried beans that were infested with weevils, and half a sack of oats.

"Well, shall we allocate ourselves duties?" Barbara asked her friends, fighting back the tears. She couldn't believe that this was going to be her life for the next two years until she turned eighteen and left the school. Would she survive until then?

"Barb, do you think anyone will remember to bring us some cake on Christmas Day?" one of the girls asked as they quickly got down to working. Barbara knew that many donations came to the school for the poor students, but these were handled by the nuns at their own discretion. Even if goodies were brought, she doubted that any would be spared for them.

"Charity, let's just be realistic and accept that all we shall have on Christmas Day is a meal of beans and oats. But just think, we're better off than so many other people who are homeless and will have to live on the streets and face the cold without proper clothing. Let's be cheerful because this is only for about ten days. When the others return, we shall taste of the goodies they will bring."

"You're lucky because you have Nancy Burton to look out for you," another student called Moira said. "We have no one to bring us goodies, unless it's something the other girls don't want," the other nodded. "Why are we treated like we're so different from them, yet they say we're in the same school?"

"Moira, we are blessed to be here," Barbara knew that one or two of the girls in their midst would definitely report their conversation to the nuns and she had to be careful about what she said. "This is a good institution, and while we're here, let's learn all we can that will help us in the future. Complaining or murmuring isn't Christian, and remember what Mother Superior has been teaching us, that we ought to be thankful for everything we have."

But she was really sad because what Moira said was true. Most of them had no one to look out for them.

"Nancy always brings a lot of stuff and I promise that I shall ask her to spare some for all of us."

The days passed swiftly and even though they had to ration their food, Barbara was glad that the nuns barely paid attention to them. They saw many carriages coming up to the castle and once in a while they were also called upon to help carry the gifts and donations to the convent but that was as far as it went. They had no idea what was brought for them but from time to time, Barbara would steal some sugar from the packages delivered and make them boiled sweets which they enjoyed.

She really longed to write to her grandmother and tell her about her life at the school but then thought better of it. In two years, Grandma Edna had never once written or visited and why should she think that this time would be any different? No, she had to accept that she had parents but was an orphan and get used to that kind of a life.

9

HIDDEN PATHS

The moment Nancy reported back to school in January, Barbara knew that something was terribly wrong. She wasn't her usual cheery self and she spent a lot of time crying and feigning illness. Because she was a privileged girl, the infirmary was open for her and Barbara was appointed to make sure that she was comfortable.

For the first week, Barbara let things slide because she thought her friend was feeling homesick. But in the second week, Barbara began to notice some very strange and disturbing changes in her friend. For one, Nancy was a very neat person and wasn't one who spat in public; she called those who did that halfwits and simpletons who loved squalor. Harsh words but which Barbara agreed with. However, she started spitting everywhere and Barbara had to keep cleaning up after her. Also, she experienced terrible nausea in the mornings.

"Something is wrong, and I want you to tell me what it is," She insisted when they had gone out to the fields. It was a cold morning, but Nancy insisted that she didn't want to be indoors. She had agreed to lend Barbara her coat and thick woollen boots for their walk.

"Barbara, I want to die," the distraught girl covered her face with her gloved palms. "Oh, I wish I could just die."

"What's wrong? Are you ill? Is it your parents? What's going on with you, Nancy?"

"No, it's not my parents and I'm not ill," the girl sobbed. "I did something terrible in the first week that I went home and now there's going to be so much trouble."

"What did you do that is so terrible? Did you kill someone?" Barbara tried to lighten the mood, but her friend just wept the more. "Nancy," she put an arm around her friend's shoulder, "I'm your friend; please tell me what is going on and how I can help."

"If my parents find out, they'll kill me, for sure," Nancy said hoarsely. "I really did a bad thing, Barbara, now my life is ruined."

"You're not making much sense to me and I really want to help you."

"Can you keep my secret?" Nancy wiped her nose with the back of her palm.

"You know that I can never tell anyone what we share in confidence. In any case, who would I even tell seeing as you're my only friend?"

"Promise me that you'll never tell anyone what I'm about to share with you."

"I promise, now tell me what's wrong so we can solve this problem. I'm sure it's something that if we put our heads together, we can come up with a solution."

Nancy was shaking her head, "Not this time, Barbara. This is going to be a terrible, lifelong mess."

"Look, the dinner gong is about to sound for you and if you're not at the table, there's no telling what Mother Superior will do to you. And I also have to go and serve my tables."

Nancy sighed, "All right then, let's go for dinner."

But Barbara held her back, "No, dinner can wait though I hope you won't get into any trouble. Look at me," she held her friend's chin gently, "Tell me what is going on or we'll be here the rest of the evening."

"Remember how I told you about that sweet young man who is our neighbour at home? The one who goes to Eton?" She twisted her lips, "He was home for the holidays at the same time as I was and came over quite a bit. I also went over to their house because our fathers are business associates."

Barbara couldn't recall the person Nancy was talking about because she always mentioned many young men whose families were friends with hers. "Yes," she said, just to get the story going. "What about him?"

"He's the worst person in the world," she sobbed.

"Why?'

"He betrayed me."

Barbara looked at her friend who wasn't making much sense. Before leaving for the Christmas holidays, Nancy had talked about her coming-out ball which her parents had promised to hold once she turned sixteen. It would give her the opportunity to meet eligible young men and begin courtship with whoever her heart chose and who considered her as worthy of being his wife.

Nancy's eyes had been dreamy as she described whatever went on during such balls because she'd attended two before for her cousins, who ended up meeting good men to marry them. She was also sure that out of the many young men she knew, a good husband would emerge. That was the reason she had also wanted Barbara to accompany her home for the Christmas holidays, so she could also meet some special young man.

"Does this young man have a name?"

"That isn't the important thing," Nancy cleared her throat and wiped her eyes. "I have to stop crying for someone who is not worthy of my tears," but her eyes filled up once again.

"What happened to the hopes you had for having a splendid coming out ball?"

"I don't want to talk about that because I was so humiliated. He came and ignored me the whole evening, dancing with Miranda Wells, at the end of which he announced that he was going to marry her."

Barbara took a deep breath, "My dear girl, you're going 'round and 'round in circles, and I know I should be annoyed at some young man for your sake but still, I thought you were meeting many more at your ball? What's so special about this particular one, even if he ignored you?"

"Oh Barbara, I wish I had stayed here in school with you, for then none of this would have happened."

"I'm sure there are more pleasant men than this particular one who was mean to you."

"He did much worse, Barb," Nancy sniffed. "We did wrong and then he turned against me and pretended like I wasn't at all important to him."

Barbara was puzzled, having no idea what her distraught friend was referring to. Nancy saw the blank look on her face and sighed. "It's terrible, Barbara," she took her friend's hand and placed it on her stomach. "Barbara, it's there."

"It's what?" Barbara touched Nancy's stomach, at first not comprehending anything. "What is . . ." then understanding suddenly dawned on her. "Oh dear! Oh dear!"

"Barbara," Nancy shook her. "Pull yourself together. I'm going to need you," she touched her stomach, "We're going to need you."

"Yes, of course," Barbara was still quite dazed at the news. Her best friend was pregnant at sixteen with a man who had abandoned her and was now marrying someone else. What did that mean for her continued stay at the school?

10

TRUTH BE TOLD

Barbara had just finished cleaning the dining room all alone when the door burst open and Mother Superior walked in. She immediately got to her feet and waited for the blow that she knew was bound to come. And she wasn't disappointed, as she held her burning cheek, she fought back the tears.

"Do you call this cleaning?" Sister Mary Claire stomped all over the floor, her muddy boots leaving prints all over the floor. "Where did I go wrong with you, Barbara? For two years, I've done all I could to shape you into a decent human being, but I've failed. The likes of you can never learn. Is there anything you can ever do right?"

Barbara now knew better than to answer back. Sister Mary Claire was clearly spoiling for a fight, but she wasn't going to give her any reason to start one. There was too much at stake here. "I'm very sorry, Mother Superior."

"You'll have to do this all over again and fast. Lunch is in one hour and I don't want the children of my good donors to have their meals delayed. They deserve so much more, and I need this place cleaned up well before they see this mess. Or else, you'll spend the rest of the afternoon working in here and I expect you to do the laundry too."

"Yes, Mother," Barbara refused to show the woman any aggravation even though she was seething inside. "I'll do it right away."

"Good," the woman said, and passing one of the two large pails Barbara was using for cleaning, she deliberately tipped it over, emptying the filthy water all over the floor.

"Nancy needs you, Baby needs you," Barbara muttered under her breath as the horrid woman gave her a mean, triumphant look before walking out of the dining hall, her thick boots making *thud* sounds as she walked away, humming a tune.

Barbara took a deep breath and got down to work. She had planned on leaving this terrible place as soon as the New Year came around, but Nancy returned from the Christmas holidays pregnant. She couldn't leave her to go through the nine months alone and so had decided to stay until they could decide what to do. Good thing was that their school uniform was made like ugly sacks that ballooned all over the place. According to the nuns, this was so they wouldn't entice any men into having immoral thoughts and falling into sin.

The frocks had worked in their favour, for Nancy was able to comfortably hide her pregnancy even though they had to bind her stomach with cloth to keep it from protruding. Barbara counted each day, wishing Nancy would be brave enough to tell her parents, but any mention of that usually sent her into fits and it would take her a while to calm down.

She was tired of always getting picked on for punishments and scorn. She worked really hard, was doing well in her lessons and had determined that she wouldn't get into any kind of trouble. For trouble meant being placed in solitary confinement, and Nancy really needed her. Yet trouble seemed to pursue her no matter how hard she tried to stay away from it.

The lunch gong sounded just as she had finished cleaning the dining hall, and she hurried to take the rugs and two pails of dirty water out before the entitled girls came pouring in. That meant slipping through the back and down a corridor that she normally wasn't allowed to use.

As she hurried toward the door at the end of the corridor that led to the backyard, she heard voices coming from one of the rooms off the corridor. She would have walked on but then heard her name mentioned.

"There's no girl in here who works as hard as Barbara Coomb, but Mother Superior seems to really hate the poor thing." She recognized the voice as belonging to a woman she only knew as Esther and who was the kitchen supervisor. "I feel sorry for some of these girls. I guess it pays to be born into a wealthy and able family because those spoilt brats are treated so much better than the others."

"Esther, you know that we're not supposed to talk about things like that for we could get into trouble," that was Martha, the woman who washed the pots and pans and usually let the poor students help so they could lick the crumbs.

"Pshaw! Don't tell me what I can or can't do. This place is supposed to provide refuge for girls as well as educate them on the finer things of life. But the rich and well-to-do are kept separate from the orphans and destitute girls. You've seen those dorms the poor girls are housed in. They are no better than barns and even farm animals would protest if they were made to stay in there. Even in medieval times, the

Lord of this Castle never let his animals stay in a draughty stable, and yet these nuns, who are supposed to have kind hearts and be God's representatives on earth are so cruel. The wealthy girls have nice beds with clean sheets that are changed every week, and it is the poor girls who do all their laundry. The poor girls live like animals in those rundown dorms because they are either orphans or their parents are too poor to give donations to the school. It's just not right in the sight of man or of God either."

Barbara thought she heard another door opening and she ducked into the nearest closet with her buckets. It was a tight fit and really dark, but this was better than being caught eavesdropping. Esther's words troubled her greatly and a lot of things began to make sense to her. When her father had dropped her off, he'd given Mother Superior a wad of notes, and her grandmother had promised that she would be well taken care of. That was when she was taken to the good and spacious dorms. But all that changed just two months later when she was dumped in the barns.

Had her parents fallen on hard times and so stopped sending money for her support? She shook her head. Grandma Edna had told her that while the family wasn't as wealthy as the Queen of England, there was still enough for them to live comfortably for many years. So, why had they stopped paying for her upkeep? Something had happened at home and more than ever, she longed to go home and make things right.

~

Mr. Alistair Bramble re-read the letter that had come to him from Fleet Street Prison nearly two years ago. He was aware that the only reason he had found the letter was because Matilda was away from home. She'd travelled to Liverpool to visit one of their cousins who'd just had a baby. It was while he was searching for something in one of the drawers of his desk and emptied it, that he'd come across the letter that had lain hidden for two years.

He loved his sister and knew that she loved him too, but she was overly protective, and though that prevented him from being taken advantage of, she also stopped him from doing his charitable works. But with her gone, he was going to take time to make up for the six years since he stopped doing so.

Lawrence Trent would be nineteen this year and not for the first time, the middle-aged man felt the tears fill up his eyes. He'd acted in anger after he recovered from the attack by Larry's father. It was all his fault and not the boy's. On the day Peter Trent had come visiting, he'd seen the stark fear in the boy's eyes and yet he'd let the man stay. The boy's terror of his own father should have made him more cautious, and after giving him a few guineas, he should have sent him away. But instead, he'd invited a viper into his house and their lives were turned upside down. It was just by the grace of God that he hadn't died that night.

With a sigh, his eyes went back to the letter from the boy he'd so wanted to help all those years back.

"Dear Mr. Alistair Bramble,

Please I beg you, don't toss this letter into the trash like I know you've done with the previous three that I wrote."

Alistair closed his eyes and took a deep breath. So, Larry had written to him on three previous occasions but clearly Matilda had kept the letters from him. He resumed reading.

"You were good to us, but we took advantage of your kindness to hurt you and for that, I'm so sorry. There are no words I can use to

tell you how sorry I am for nearly causing your death. I just pray that you will find it in your heart to forgive us.

My family and I have more than paid for our sins, and this is my humble request to you, Sir, that you would pardon our sins and grant us our freedom. You see, when we entered this prison, there were seven of us. But in the span of six years, my four little siblings, who were innocent of any crimes, all died due to cholera, dysentery, and typhoid. Prison isn't a place for children, Sir. I know that it's our own fault that we're here, but I throw myself on your mercy. I also make a promise to you that should you grant me a pardon, I will work hard doing only legal work and half my wages will go toward paying what was stolen from you. Even if it takes me my whole life, I promise that I will make good on this, kind Sir.

My father died just a few weeks ago, and now my mother is seriously ill. If you pardon our sin, I shall be able to find a doctor to treat her. She's the only one I have left right now, and I'm pleading for her life and mine, Sir.

I'll be waiting to hear back from you, hoping that your mercy will trump your justice.

Yours faithfully,

Lawrence Trent."

By the time he finished reading the letter, Alistair was sobbing loudly. He was glad that he was alone in his study for then he could let his emotions free. It was a long while before he was calm enough to reach for pen and paper to write down his pardon to the family that he had destroyed because of his anger. May God forgive me, he murmured as he penned the pardon.

11

BEHIND CLOSED DOORS

It had rained heavily the night before and the paths leading from the barn to the cobbled courtyard were muddy and pools of water had formed where the stones had loosened up. Getting from one side of the courtyard to the other was difficult but something had come upon the Mother Superior that morning and she made all the girls from both sides, assemble there. It was still drizzling but the nun kept the girls outside for reasons best known to herself.

Barbara was worried about Nancy, whose face was quite pale. By her count, her friend was due to have her baby any day now. The past nine months had been extremely challenging for both of them but at no point had Barbara complained. She was doing all this for Nancy who had been good to her for the past two years and nine months and treated her like a sister.

"Barb, I don't feel so good," Nancy hang at the back, behind one of the pillars.

"Do you think it's time?"

"Maybe," she leaned heavily against the wall and the girls around were staring curiously at her. Barbara glared at them and they hastily averted their gazes. It was well known that no one joked around with Barbara or Nancy. Even if they reported her to the Mother Superior, she would always find a way of getting back at them, so most of the girls learned to steer clear of her.

"I need to go to the infirmary."

"No, you can't do that. Remember we talked about this, that when the time comes, we would find our way to the old shed. Otherwise, things might get really bad for us and for the baby."

"I know, but I'm really afraid," Nancy bent over, and a soft moan escaped her lips. "The pain is killing me; it's ripping me apart."

That decided it for Barbara. "We're going to the shed."

"But it's started raining so hard now."

"The better for us. See, everyone is hurrying out of the rain to seek shelter and that means no one will bother about us. Are you able to walk on your own?'

"I'll try," Nancy said but remained bent over. "Just let this pain ease up a little bit."

"I wish there was something I could do to make you feel better, Nancy."

Nancy gave a small laugh, "My dearest friend, you've done so much for me and this baby these past nine months that I don't know how I'll ever repay you. Anyone else would have left me to face this all alone and who knows what might have happened to me?'

"Nancy, you've also been good to me since I set foot in this place," they paused for a while and then Nancy straightened up.

"Let's go, I can now walk."

"Okay, follow me, and if we meet anyone, we'll simply say we're going to the outhouse."

"Lead the way."

The old shed was an abandoned shack where all the old furniture from the convent, the classes, and the dorms was tossed. From here, the wood cutter would turn it into fuel for the kitchen fire. Being a large shed that had seemingly once been another barn, it was full of broken tables, chairs, chests, and beds, and it would be a while before anyone found them. Barbara hoped that by then, Nancy's baby would have been born and they could hide it.

She had found this place by accident when she was put on punishment by the Mother Superior over some flimsy reason. On that day, the woodcutter had been indisposed because of what he claimed was a weak stomach but which Barbara knew to be a drunken stupor. She had found his stash of moonshine buried in the shed on one of her trips there. The cooks had needed firewood and since she was on punishment, Barbara was forced to go into the shed and split some old furniture to be used in the kitchen.

With her usual curiosity, she'd spent considerable time in there when the thought came to her about making this the place where Nancy would have her baby without anyone being the wiser. And so, in the months leading up to the present, she'd prepared an area at the back of the furniture and it would be hard for anyone to find them, especially now that it was raining so hard and there was so much thunder and lightning.

"Come," Barbara led the way into the shed, moved a few bits and pieces of furniture and revealed the secret passageway that she had created. There was a clean mattress lying on a bed that had three legs. To make it stable, Barbara had it leaning against the wall and she'd pushed some wood under to reinforce it. She had stolen the mattress from the lawn during summer when they had to turn everything out for airing. She had also managed to get blankets and sheets, some of which she tore into reasonable squares to act as diapers for the baby.

"I think this baby is coming," Nancy announced as there was a splash from between her legs. "My water just broke."

"Quick, get on the bed and lie down."

"Do you know what to do?" Nancy clutched her hand as she lay on the pillow. "I don't want anything to happen to my baby." Even in her pain, Nancy loved the child that would change her life forever. She had stopped saying mean things about the man who put her in the family way and over the months, had concentrated on getting ready for her baby.

"Of course, I know what to do," Barbara said with far more confidence than she was feeling. She'd only seen a woman having a baby once and that was when she was twelve years old. "Just try to relax and also, you can scream as loud as you want. No one will hear you above the noise of thunder, lightning, and rain.

A peal of thunder exploded above them but instead of being frightened, Barbara sent a prayer of gratitude heavenward. The loud noise outside masked the loud screams of pain inside the shed.

"Then let's bring my baby into the world," Nancy said, her eyes serious.

Walking from the prison to the outer courtyard and toward the gate felt like a dream for Larry. He stopped and raised his face to the sky. He was free, Mr. Alistair had finally granted him a pardon. It was two years after he'd written his last letter and given up hope, but just this morning, one of the guards had informed him that he was a free man.

Still expecting to be shouted at and called back, he took slow steps towards the gate. He could see a fancy carriage waiting there and at first didn't pay much attention to it. But when he stepped out of the gates and saw the man standing there, he stopped.

Mr. Alistair Bramble had more grey hair than when Larry had last seen him, but he still had the same kind eyes. There was also a deep scar on his forehead, where Larry's father had struck him, and the young man bowed his head in shame.

"Larry," Mr. Alistair walked slowly towards him. "I'm so sorry that it's taken this long to get you released. The warden told me that your mother died two years ago."

"Mr. Alistair, I can barely face you for the shame I feel."

"I've come to take you back home so we can start again," Mr. Alistair said but Larry shook his head. He couldn't bear to go into that home and see the spot where his benefactor had lain for hours after his own father had tried to kill him. "Larry, I said I'm sorry."

"Mr. Alistair, please forgive me but I'm unworthy of your benevolence. Please Sir, thank you for setting me free and I promise that I will pay back every penny that my father took from you."

It was Alistair's turn to shake his head, "When I pardoned you, I also forgave the debt in totality. You owe me nothing, and all I want is for you to go out into the world and have a good life. I'm ready to do anything to make up for the six years that you were wrongfully imprisoned. If anything, I'm in your debt for reacting angrily when you, your mother and siblings weren't at fault."

"We deserved it for taking advantage of you, Sir."

"Larry, I don't want you to blame yourself for whatever happened. Shall we leave all that in the past and move forward? What can I do to make things right for you?"

Larry thought for a moment then smiled, "Mr. Alistair, I know that my request is going to sound rather unusual."

"Go on, tell me what it is you want."

"In there," he pointed over his shoulder at the prison, "I met a family. Their name is Smith. A travelling salesman left a stove in their home, but they didn't want it. When the man demanded to be paid, they didn't have the money, so he had them brought to prison. Sir, it's a man, his wife and their four children. Please, for the sake of those little ones, if there's anything you can do to help them, you can consider your debt to me repaid in full."

Alistair smiled, "Say no more and consider it done. Would you like to come with me as we speak to the family to get all the facts right?"

"Yes, Sir."

12

UP IN FLAMES

He was beautiful and the two friends wept over him, "Nancy, you're really going to be a wonderful mother. He is so beautiful, and I just want to hold him and keep him safe," Barbara kissed the little boy's forehead. "Have you decided on a name for him?"

Nancy nodded, "Clifford. That's my Papa's middle name," she added quickly when she saw Barbara's questioning look. "But he has green eyes and carrot red hair just like . . ." her voice trailed away. She blushed and turned her face away. Barbara knew she was thinking about the man who had put her in this situation. Her lips tightened as she thought about her friend's pain in the past nine months.

Nancy had written so many letters to the father of her son but hadn't received a single response from him. There were days when she would make all kinds of excuses for the man and then there were days when she would weep and pronounce curses upon his head.

"You'll be all right, Nancy, you and Clifford."

"No, I won't. My parents will never accept this child because I have brought shame to them. And if the nuns find out about him, they will take him away from me and I'll never see him again."

"I'll take him," Barbara found herself saying.

"Where, how? What do you mean you'll take him?"

Barbara gave a small laugh, "I had planned on escaping from this place just after everyone else returned from Christmas holidays. But then you came and told me about your situation, and I knew I couldn't leave you to face this whole thing alone. So, I stayed and took care of you, but now there's no need for me to continue staying here. So, I'll take your son and go."

"You're a good friend, but how will you get out and where will you go?"

Barbara smiled, "I'm going home to see my grandmother and my brother. When I left home, my grandmother promised that she would write to me and also visit, but I've been here for two years and nine months now and she has never come to see me or even written once. But she loves me, and I know she'll know what to do."

"Are you sure?" Nancy's arms tightened around her baby. She didn't want to remind her friend that her so-called beloved grandmother had never once visited or written to her. What made her think that the woman would welcome her home and with a child in tow? "What if she insists on you putting my baby in a foundling home and then sending you back here?"

"First, I'm not coming back here, no matter what anyone says. Believe me, Grandma loves me so much, and when she finds out how I've been treated here, she will never allow my parents to bring me back. She will also not let Clifford be taken to the orphanage or anywhere else. Nancy, I'll keep your son safe until you can come for him."

"Please, don't let anyone take my baby away. I'll think about what to do and will come back to find you and Clifford."

"Don't worry about us at all, we'll be fine and counting the days until we can see you again."

"But how will you get away? This place is like a fortress and we're surrounded on every side by thick woods."

"Tomorrow is Tuesday, the day when the old farmer brings fresh produce to the convent and school. I know that because one of my duties as head of the riff raff, as the Mother Superior calls me, insists on me helping him to offload the cart. He's half blind and I'll wait until his back is turned and sneak onto his cart. But I will still need your help, that's if you can walk."

"Whatever you want."

"I'll need someone to distract the people in the kitchen and keep them busy until we can get away."

"Consider it done." Nancy winced as she tried to sit up and nurse her son. "I have to nurse him as much as I can until tomorrow."

"We'll both spend the night here and I'll be gone by dawn to make sure the old farmer has come by."

"How will you hide Clifford?"

"I'll have him strapped to my chest and good thing is that it's the rainy season and it's very cold. That gives me the excuse to have the thick coat on. Make sure you cause as much distraction as possible."

"Please Lord, let this work," Barbara prayed as she her eyes darted to and fro, looking out for any kind of trouble. The baby was asleep, but the old farmer was still haggling over the price of potatoes. She couldn't hear much of what was being said but she hoped Nancy would keep everyone occupied long enough for them to leave.

As she was crouching behind a small bush waiting for the farmer to finish offloading the cart, she checked on the baby. He was still sleeping. Nancy had fed him for most of the night and then provided some milk in a bottle so Barbara could carry a little extra with her.

She thought she heard a scream but couldn't be sure. All she saw was the old farmer coming out, hauling another bag of potatoes, the last one and then stomping back into the kitchen. That was the chance she was waiting for and quickly climbed up the cart and dove under the empty sacks. All she had to do was get to Wolverton or close enough to walk to the railway station and board the next train to Bletchley.

A few minutes later, she felt the cart rattling and the old man muttering to himself. But she couldn't rejoice just yet since the old man's mule was as old and slow as himself.

But at last they were moving, she thought, as the gentle rocking of the cart lulled her to sleep. Her legs were cramped and her left arm stiff from lying on it for so long, but Clifford would be safe. Grandma would make sure that they were.

Once the Smith family were freed and returned to their house, Larry felt that his work was done.

"I have to leave London for a while," he told Mr. Alistair who hadn't stopped pleading with him to return to the house. "Thank you for all that you've done for me and for that family, Sir."

"You were a good boy when I met you nine years ago and have grown up into a fine young man, Larry. I just wish you would accept my offer."

"Sir, to be honest, I would love nothing more than to return and work for you. But Miss Matilda was badly affected by what happened, and I'm afraid that our relationship will never be what it was before. That will make it very uncomfortable for all of us to live together, and I prefer that I should go far away and find something to do."

"Well, if you insist, at least allow me to send you to the home of an acquaintance out in Cheddington. It's out of London but not so far that you can't return should you ever want to. The man's name is Weldon Summers and he has a dairy farm out there. Just tell him that I sent you and he'll give you work to do. Here," he placed twenty pounds in Larry's hand. "This will be enough for your transport as well as enable you to find a place to stay for a few days until you can settle down."

Larry wanted to cry when he got to Mr. Summers's home, only to be informed that the man had died a few months before. His widow was still young and the looks she gave Larry made him quite uncomfortable, even in the presence of her two sons who were teenagers.

"You'll make a fine young addition to my household," The Widow Summers told him, but he shook his head.

"Mr. Alistair told me that if I don't find Mr. Summers, then I should return to London immediately and inform him," he lied. "Thank you very much for the kind offer, Ma'am."

And he quickly left before the woman had any chance of detaining him there for whatever reason. His mother's words were forever stuck in his mind. The Widow Summers was wealthy and even though the temptation of having an easy life after the tough six years in prison was there, he loved his mother too much to succumb. Besides, his own father had gotten involved with wealthy widows and that had led him down a terrible path.

No, he would work hard with his own hands and earn a living, so that his mother would be proud of him. He had made her the promise, and he would keep it.

It was while he was walking around Cheddington that he saw the advertisement on the wall of a grocery store. A Mr. Graham needed a stable boy and groundsman and the advert said that any interested person should ask in the store. So, he pushed open the door and entered.

"Son, if you need anything, you have to wait for the Missus to return," a voice hailed him. "My hand is injured, and I can't be of much help to you."

"Sir, I'm here because of the advertisement that is outside. It says that anyone who is interested should ask in here."

"That Graham man," the storekeeper chuckled. "I don't know if you'll last longer than the other young men who've been there. The man is difficult to deal with, I tell you."

"I'm a hard worker and I really need a job and somewhere to live."

"I'll send you there for I can see that you're a good young man. But stay away from the man's wife or he'll toss you out on your ear. She's a pretty young thing and much younger than him so the man gets insanely jealous if anyone as much as looks in her direction."

"I understand, Sir."

"Now, go down that road . . ." and Larry listened keenly as he was given directions to the Graham Farm. It was about four miles out of the town centre, and for him that was not an issue. He needed to be in a place where he didn't have to come in contact with anyone who might draw him away from his purpose.

He intended to work hard and one day buy a small farm where he would settle down and live for the rest of his life. He was done with London and other towns where the temptations were great and trouble waited in the wings to pounce upon the unsuspecting.

13

JUST AN ILLUSION

This was all too much to take in. All her life until now had just been an illusion, not real; and just like illusions tended to fade away when reality struck, so had all her dreams and hopes.

Barbara didn't even notice the rain as it fell around her, eyes being fixed on the large gate she wanted to walk through and leave forever.

What hurt most was finding out that her grandmother had died just two weeks after she left for school. Her beloved Grandma had been dead for two years and nine months, but no one had thought it important to let her know. Not even Toby, her beloved brother.

Well, it was now all clear to her why she had always felt like her parents didn't love her. They were not her birth parents and Grandma Edna was not even related to her.

"Your grandmother, the real one was called Ingrid Foster. She was my mother's best friend from childhood. After you were born, your mother became ill and passed away just weeks later. No one knows what happened to your father after your mother died. Your grandmother took you in, but she was also ill, and when you were two and a half years old, Mrs. Ingrid Foster died. She wrote to my mother telling her that she was dying and needed her help. My mother found you in the care of some people and took you away, bringing you into our home," Mr. Gilbert Coomb, the man she had believed was her father had been so cold as he delivered blow upon blow. "My mother brought you here when you were just about three years old and forced us to adopt you. Because we depended on her for our livelihood, we silently took you in even though it wasn't something we wanted to do. But you're not a part of this family and our obligation toward you ended with my mother's death over two years ago."

That had made things very clear to Barbara. No wonder her life at St. Agatha's had suddenly changed for the worse. Mr. Coomb had stopped paying for her upkeep, so the nuns treated her like one of the destitute girls.

"What's even worse is you returning to this house after playing the harlot with some village lout and expecting us to take you in with your baseborn baby. Did you think you could just behave in any way you want and then come back here and be accepted?" Janice hissed at her. "Thank God you're not our child or even related to us or we would never live this shame down."

"I'm sorry," she bowed her head. "I'll go and leave you in peace. Please forgive me for all the wrong I've done to you."

"You can stay the night because it's raining heavily and we're not monsters," Mr. Coomb said. "But you'll have to go to the servants' quarters because you're not a member of this family. I want you gone from my house in the morning or I'll get the village constable to take you out of here by force."

Barbara had turned to the one person she thought might be on her side. In the two years since she'd last seen him, Toby had really grown into a man. He was taller than she remembered and looked so handsome.

But there was no smile for her on his lips and his eyes were as cold as his father's. He didn't even speak a single word, but turned and walked away. Before he closed the door behind him, he turned, and their eyes met once more. This time, she saw hurt and disappointment and wished she could tell him the truth about Clifford. But she held her peace, knowing that even if these people she'd always thought were her parents didn't want her, they could hurt Clifford too.

She left the house and decided to leave but was now standing in front of the large iron gates, wondering if she should just walk away. This was no longer her home and she would be gone in the morning anyway. But she had Clifford to consider. The night was going to get colder and the starless sky promised more rain.

"Child, what are you doing out here?" Maurice the old stable man came out of nowhere, startling her. "Mrs. Hunter heard you in the drawing room and then she saw you leave the house. Were you intending to go away in this darkness?"

"I thought about it."

"I know your grandmother wouldn't want you to put the life of that child at risk. Come," he took her bag from her, "Let's go and get you into a warm place and find you something to eat."

Barbara allowed herself to be led back to the house but this time, through the back and into the kitchen.

It was funny that the only people in this house where she'd grown up who were kind to her, were the servants.

Cookie was immediately at her side and she fussed over Clifford, holding him close. "You have a beautiful boy, Barbara. It's a pity what you're going through. If your grandmother were still alive, she would be over the moon about her great grandson."

Barbara just smiled sadly, tears rolling down her cheeks.

"Child, it can't be that bad."

"I just miss Grandma so much. When I went to school and she never wrote back or came to visit as she had promised, I was angry. In my mind, Grandma had abandoned me, and I blamed her for not caring about me. And yet, she was dead and buried all this time, and no one, not even Toby, told me," Barbara bowed her head and wept.

"Your grandmother loved you. She talked about you even in her final moments," Cookie said. "She was so proud of you and her one regret was that she wouldn't be there to see you grow."

"Then why did she send me away," Barbara sobbed brokenly. "I knew she was ill, but I didn't think it was that serious. Before I left, I begged her not to let my parents, er, Mr. and Mrs. Coomb, send me away, but she still let it happen."

Cookie shook her head, "I wish there was something I could do or say to make you feel better, but I don't have any answers for you."

14
AN UNCLEAR DREAM

Barbara could hear the other servants chatting through the slightly opened door. She felt that she had imposed enough on their generosity and didn't want them getting into any kind of trouble because of her. They had done enough for her, and Megan had even given up her bed because of Clifford.

The one thing that made her smile in all this was finding out that Anne, Cookie's daughter, was now married to a nice young man who had accepted her even though she had a child. He was a carpenter and, according to Cookie, they were living a wonderful life.

"Or else I wouldn't have let my Little Anne marry him. It's a good thing the other lout abandoned her for she now found a wonderful man to love and cherish her," the cook had said. "Which is why I want you to wipe away your tears, child. The good Lord will bring you a man along your way and he will wipe away the tears the other one caused. Some men are just good that way."

Barbara had spent nearly half the night thinking about the cook's words. Would she ever find a good man to love and accept her, or would he want to know much about her past?

But now she had to leave and find her way to Nancy's home before the owners of the house caused trouble for the servants. Janice, the woman she had always called mother wasn't very kind to the servants and it was her grandmother who had kept things running smoothly in this household.

Clifford stirred and she shushed him as she strapped him to her chest. Picking up her battered carpetbag, she slipped out through the empty kitchen and into the backyard. She could hear one of the stable boys whistling tunelessly inside the stable and felt more pain. More than anything, she longed to go into the stable and take a peek at Moonlight, the pony her grandmother had bought her for her thirteenth birthday.

Then she shook her head; she was going to have to stop referring to Edna as her grandmother because she wasn't. But how does a person just cancel out years of love and care? Barbara shook her head again. No, Edna would always be her grandmother even if her family had refused to accept her. Some bonds were just too strong to break, and not even pain and abandonment could rip them apart.

Before she left, however, she had to bid farewell to that very special and beloved woman. In the past, Edna had taken her to the family cemetery plot at the edge of the estate.

"When I die, this is where I'll be buried," she had pointed at a certain spot under a large elm tree. "Next to my parents; and when all of you die, you'll join us here."

"What about Grandfather Coomb?" Barbara had ventured to ask because she didn't see Arthur Coomb's tombstone anywhere.

"He died at sea, so there was no body to bury."

But even with that hasty explanation, Barbara had always felt that her grandmother was hiding something because she never talked about her husband, Arthur.

No one noticed her as she walked down the cobbled path toward the garden and beyond. The clouds were dark and heavy, and she knew that a downpour was imminent.

"Clifford, we have come this far, but we need to keep moving," at least he was fed and dry. Cookie had sent Megan to grab a few things up from the attic, baby things that had belonged to Toby.

Barbara had always wondered why there were no baby clothes for her up in the large trunk in the attic. Now she knew and twisted her lips. The bag she carried on her shoulder was heavy but she needed to see Grandma's grave for the first and last time so she could bid her farewell.

Just like she'd always said, Grandma Edna was buried next to her parents who shared the same grave. As Barbara stood there looking down at the tombstone, she allowed the tears to fall freely.

"Oh Grandma," she sobbed. "I'm so sorry I wasn't here for you in the end. I'm sorry for being angry and thinking that you had abandoned me," she gave a sad laugh. "Well, in a way, you did. My father admitted—no, I shouldn't call him that because he said not to. They say I will bring them shame if I stay, and they are right. Any obligation toward me ended with your death, and as far as they are concerned, I don't belong here. But I have Clifford to take care of now and that's what I'm going to do. I'll be strong like you always taught me to be, and one day, I will make you proud of me, Grandma." She sank to her knees on the wet grass. "Oh Grandma, I miss you so much that it hurts. I wish I could stay here all day and talk to you but I have to go to Leighton and find my best friend Nancy's parents so they can take responsibility for their grandson. I know that they too will be hurt by what she did, but she was just a foolish child in love, who did the wrong thing. You used to tell me all the time that it is good to be merciful even when people make mistakes." Clifford stirred but didn't wake up. "You would have loved Clifford. He's such a lovely child who should be with his Mama right now. I'm taking him to Mr. and Mrs. Burton so they can take care of him. After that, I'll find a household where I can work as a housekeeper and save money to one day open up my own candy store. I'll call it Edna's Candy Store in your honour, for you were the one who taught me how to make all those sweet delights. Remember how we used to talk about it for hours? When I have saved enough money, I'll find a nice town, maybe even London, and set up my shop. You were good to me, Grandma, and I will always love you. Thank you for everything, for loving me and opening up your home to me even though you didn't have to." She bent over the grave and wept for a long while.

Just as she was about to leave, she noticed that the earth at the head of the grave right under the tombstone was freshly dug. "Moles," she murmured and started to turn away but then noticed something else. A small tin was partly buried in the newly dug hole and she bent closer to find out what it was. Then she smiled; it was the same tin Toby had used to put his pennies in for years. He used to call it his bank and anytime they got a penny from their grandmother or parents, he would put his in there.

Heart pounding, she reached for the tin and opened it. Then she gasped. There were two gold sovereigns in it. Was this where he now hid his money or was this some kind of a message to her?

Whatever the case, she now had some money to pay for her journey to Leighton. She would beg the Burtons to let her stay with them and help take care of Clifford until his mother came home. But would they believe her when she told them that the baby was Nancy's, or would they think she was some mad girl out to fleece them? She would just have to find a way to convince them.

"Thank you, Toby," she said to the wind and rose to her feet. Straightening the baby on her chest and picking up her bag, she walked away with a lighter heart and feet.

Once he was satisfied that Barbara had found the money he'd intended for her, Toby crept back to the house before his parents woke up.

He had paid his debt to his grandmother, he thought. Then why did he still feel like he'd let her down, let both of them down?

15

TRUTH BEHIND THE MASK

"This is as far as I can go, Miss," the old farmer told her. "The rains have made the paths impassable but the house you seek is just about a mile down that road," and he pointed in the said direction.

"Thank you," Barbara tried not to look so dismayed. The path the man had indicated was muddy and there were puddles of water all over.

It was hard to believe that less than two weeks had passed since she'd left the convent. It seemed like a lifetime ago but thankfully, her journey was about to come to an end. She would beg and plead with Nancy's parents to take their grandson in. This boy deserved to have a good home, a warm cot to sleep in every night and enough nourishment. As she trudged along the road, trying very hard to avoid the mud, she was careful not to walk too fast. The last thing she wanted was for her to fall down. Clifford was wet and his diaper needed to be changed, and he was starting to fuss. Besides that, she was cold and hungry.

The two sovereigns she'd found at her grandmother's grave were all but gone, what with spending three nights in an inn because she was worried that Clifford had been coming down with a cold. Mercifully, it turned out to be nothing, but the lovely lady at the inn had provided her with enough goat's milk to feed him with. Then, she had spent more on the train fare down to Leighton and finally hired the old man's cart to convey her to her destination. But he'd left her halfway after pocketing her money.

Clifford sniffed, "My love, just a few yards and we'll be there," she told him. Even though she was coming to the Burton's home, she didn't have too many expectations like when she'd been going home. Then, she'd envisioned her grandmother receiving her with a warm embrace, then calling for hot tea to be brought to her and for one of the servants to take the baby and attend to him. She had seen in her mind's eye her grandmother sending one of the servants to prepare her old bedroom and maybe bring down a crib from the attic for Clifford, and then listening to her as she told her all that had happened.

None of that had happened, however, and she was more cautious now. A baby may be a blessing to most families but not in the way Nancy had had Clifford. She was more cautious, no need to hope for something that might not happen.

While she knew Nancy's parents to be kind people, there was no telling how they would react to the presence of a baby in their home, their sixteen-year-old unmarried daughter's child.

"Clifford, I'm praying that your grandparents will at least accept to receive you into their home. After all, you're their flesh and blood," but even as she spoke to the child, her heart was unsettled.

The rumbling sound of a carriage coming her way from up ahead made her hastily leave the road and head for the hedge. Even though there were many houses around her, they were nestled a distance away from the deserted road, and she was afraid of falling prey to some bad people.

Even though most highway robberies occurred on the main road to London, there were also reports of people being attacked and robbed on deserted country roads. And for a woman alone, things could even turn out to be worse.

Barbara crouched behind one of the hedges when she realized that what she'd heard was more than one carriage coming down the road. In fact, she counted seven of them and when the last one had gone by and she was sure no other was coming, she rose and stared at them as they disappeared in the distance. It was clear that the coachmen driving them were hurrying to take their occupants back home, out of the cold weather and into their warm houses.

Many carriages travelling together usually meant a wedding or a funeral. "Well," she shrugged, resuming her journey once again, "Whatever has taken place has nothing to do with me." She was hungry and so was Clifford, who was making small cat like sounds. He was also sniffing her dress front, clearly seeking nourishment. "Oh my love, I wish I could provide what you need," she told him. He began whimpering as if he understood what she was saying. "We'll be there shortly."

It was nearly two hours before she got to her destination. Just like the old man had told her, the Burtons' home wasn't that far from where he'd dropped her off. But trudging carefully through the mud, stopping from time to time to wipe her feet and also being careful not to fall had made the journey very slow.

It started drizzling as she slipped through the large gates that for some reason were standing open and unattended. That gave her a funny feeling in her stomach, remembering that when that had happened back at home, they'd been entertaining.

The Burtons' residence was an old rambling house that looked so welcoming in the gloomy weather. It had two stories but what surprised Barbara was that all the curtains on the top floor seemed to be drawn even though it was only mid morning. This looked like the kind of house that always had its windows open with laughter filling every room, and she could envision her friend living here. But for now, all was quiet, eerily quiet.

Then she noticed the many carriage wheel tracks and wondered if the seven that had passed her a while back had been here. That seemed to be the case.

No one hailed or stopped her when she walked up to the large wooden door and used the brass knocker, tapping it three times. She heard footsteps as if coming from afar but finally the bolts were pushed back and the door opened.

"Yes, Miss?" The woman who stood there was in her mid fifties and her eyes were red, as if she had a cold or had been crying.

"My name is Barbara and I've come a long way."

"Clearly," the woman stared pointedly at her muddy shoes. "Did you walk down the road?" Her eyes were suspicious as they settled on Barbara, and not overly welcoming.

"Yes, the old farmer refused to bring me any further," Barbara said.

"That must be Old Angus, one gloomy man."

"He didn't talk much. May I please speak with Mr. And Mrs. Burton?" Her words were met with a long silence that unnerved her.

"Where are you from?" The woman heard Clifford's cry and her stern features softened. "You have a little one."

"Yes, Ma'am, his name is Clifford. It's because of him that I'm here to see Mr. and Mrs. Burton." She turned to look toward the gate. A lone guard was shutting them now. "I noticed that they were entertaining and don't want to bother them but it's rather urgent, if you don't mind."

The woman shook her head slowly, tears coursing down her cheeks again. "Miss, I'm afraid you're too late," and her voice broke. She moved away from the doorway and waved Barbara in. "Please come in and forgive me but I'm so distraught. It's been a terrible week here in this house."

Barbara kicked her muddy shoes off and left them outside as she stepped into the large, warm living room. There was a fire burning in the hearth and she longed to go close and hold out her frozen hands to it. But the woman led her to a chair which she gratefully sank into.

"Miss, if you came down the road then you must have noticed the carriages."

"Yes, Ma'am."

"Yes, we had guests but not in the way you think. They were here to attend the burials of Mr. and Mrs. Burton and their daughter."

Barbara wasn't aware that Nancy had a sister, and the news about the deaths of her parents shocked her.

"Mr. and Mrs. Burton contracted typhoid and cholera when they travelled to London a few weeks back, but they didn't think it was that serious. The terrible weather affected them when they got back home, and they died a few days later, within hours of each other." She bowed her head and Barbara saw her shoulders shaking. "We had barely gotten over the shock of their deaths, when we received news from St. Agatha where their daughter Nancy is in school that her dormitory caught fire and she was one of those who was burned to death." The woman covered her face and sobbed loudly, unaware of the blow that she'd just delivered. "Such a tragedy, wiping out the whole family," and she crossed herself religiously. "It's a curse, I tell you."

All Barbara could think about was that Nancy was dead and any hope of meeting her parents was also gone. How could that be? She'd only been with her less than two weeks ago.

"Are you sure about Nancy?" She ventured to ask.

"Oh Child, did you know her?" The woman noticed her stricken look. "

"Yes," Barbara whispered, "She was my best friend in school until," she looked down at Clifford.

The woman misunderstood her and nodded slowly, "Some wicked man put you in the family way and left you to fend for yourself, so you had to leave the convent. You poor thing, and how kind of Nancy to have sent you to her parents so they would help you." She rose to her feet, "Sorry, I forget my manners, but you can understand that with all that's been going on these past few days, I'm quite beside myself. My name is Florence and I'm the housekeeper here or was," she twisted her lips wryly. "This place is going to be locked up until the solicitor decides what to do with it. Seeing as the Burtons had only one child who is now buried beside them, a relative will have to be found to take it over. I'm not sure if the person who comes in will want staff because they may bring their own. Mr. Wagner, the solicitor, came by yesterday and settled all the servants' wages and pensions, then told us that we had to leave as soon as the burials were over."

Barbara still couldn't believe that her best friend was dead. "What happened to Nancy?" She needed to know everything.

"Miss Nancy and twenty other girls were asleep in the dormitory when it caught fire, and this was five days ago. We'd been expecting her to come home and bury her parents when we got the news. The school sent over her remains so she could be buried with her parents. It's so sad."

The gruesome news finally sank in and Barbara gave a wail and collapsed. If Florence hadn't moved swiftly, the baby would have fallen on the floor. She grabbed him and hastily stepped aside as Barbara slid to the floor in a dead faint.

"Oh dear," was all Florence could mutter as she fluttered around, trying to calm the wailing child while taking care of the unconscious girl at the same time.

16

AS LONG AS WE LOVE

arbara stayed at the Burtons' residence for two days before she decided to leave. She was aware that it was her presence at the house that was preventing Florence from leaving. All the other servants, except for two guards, had already left for new postings or to be with their families as they thought about what to do now that they were no longer employed.

"Where will you go with your baby?" Florence asked her.

"I don't know." Everything seemed surreal and early that morning, she'd stood at Nancy's graveside and made a silent promise to her friend that she would take care of Clifford, no matter what. If only Nancy had told her the name of her son's father, she sighed. It was too late now and there was no use lamenting over what she couldn't control.

"My sister works in Cheddington for a good family. A few days ago, she sent me an urgent message that they need a scullery maid and asked me to find one for the household. I haven't responded to her letter yet. Do you think you can go down there and work?"

"Will they allow me to keep my baby?"

"That, I don't know but if you wish, I can take you there then we'll find out more. But wouldn't it be better if you took your child to your family and left him there? Most households I know don't hire maids with babies."

"Clifford stays with me," Barbara said firmly. "My parents are dead, and I don't have any relatives to leave him with else that's where I would be. I was hoping that Mr. And Mrs. Burton would help me."

"I'm sure we will be able to work something out. I really feel sad for you, Barbara, and for your baby. My employers would have taken you in right away because they were very kind people. They would have given you a home until you were ready to stand on your own two feet. But unfortunately, they're gone."

"Mrs. Florence, I can't thank you enough for your kindness even though you didn't know me. May God reward you bountifully."

"Thank you, too," she smiled. "Now, shall we prepare ourselves to go to my sister's place? Her name is Emelda and she's older than me but she's also a good soul."

Emelda Franklin turned out to be the housekeeper of a family that lived in a nice country house. Barbara found herself wishing she would be allowed to stay. The weather was terrible, and she was glad when she was welcomed into a warm kitchen. When Emelda told her that she could keep her baby as long as he was quiet and didn't interfere with her work, she burst into tears and thanked the two women over and over again.

"Pull yourself together, girl," Emelda told her. "Make sure you don't slacken in your duties otherwise you'll be asked to leave. But I must ask you something before we finalise this matter," she said.

"What is it, Mrs. Emelda?"

"I know that I'm considering giving you this job but seeing as you're just a child yourself, why don't you consider taking your baby to an orphanage and leaving him there? Many places will take in this beautiful boy and I can even refer you to one right here in Cheddington. They will take care of him and if you commit to paying them for his upkeep, they will not give him up for adoption or fostering and when your lot changes, you can always go and get him back."

Barbara didn't know why the woman's words troubled her. It was a good idea and one she should consider, but she found herself shaking her head. Unlike Florence, even though Emelda seemed pleasant, there was something about her that made Barbara uncomfortable. But she needed work and a place to stay until she had thought things through.

"I promise, Mrs. Emelda, my son won't be any trouble and I'll work with him strapped to my back if need be."

"Make sure that Mr. and Mrs. Sutter don't find out about him. I don't want any trouble."

"Yes, Ma'am."

~

Working in the Sutter Household was hard. They entertained three times a week even though the weather was terrible, and it rained all the time. It would take her hours to clean up the dishes and keep the kitchen clean, only to have to repeat everything all over again after the next party.

She also had no idea just how beautiful she was and never noticed the troubled looks Emelda gave her.

"Make sure that you never go beyond this door," the housekeeper pointed at the door that led from the kitchen to the rest of the house. "Your work as a scullery maid is to wash all the dishes, pots and pans, and help the cook. Is that understood?"

"Yes, Ma'am."

"The day that you cross this threshold is the day I'll have you packing your bags to leave. The family don't like mixing with servants and especially not the scullery maid. Stay in your own part of the house, is that understood?"

"Yes, Mrs. Emelda."

Even though Barbara was glad to have a job, she was saddened by the treatment she got. In this household where there was plenty of food, she was practically starving because she wasn't allowed to eat until the family and their visitors had had their fill. And even then, all the food that came back from the master's table soon disappeared into pails as cook and her two daughters who worked as chambermaids took it all away. They barely left anything for her to eat, so she had to make do with what she could scrape from the pots and pans that she cleaned.

"Clifford," she told her son one night when her growling stomach was keeping her awake. "I promise you that as soon as I make enough money, we'll leave this place and find somewhere better."

Her room was nothing more than a closet, and since a bed couldn't fit in it, all she had was a straw mattress to sleep on. She had to change the straw every few days because of the dampness, and it wasn't always easy to get fresh straw from the stables. The stable boys made her uncomfortable with their lewd remarks. One even offered her his bed above the stables, but she ignored them.

Feeding Clifford was even harder and each day she prayed that her son, for that was how she thought of him, wouldn't die of hunger. She would chew whatever food was available and then feed him like the birds did. There wasn't any milk to spare in the household and the only days that she got enough for both of them was when Cook made oatmeal porridge.

The children of the house, who were in their twenties, didn't like oatmeal porridge and neither did cook and her daughters. But Mrs. Sutter insisted on it being prepared twice a week even though the jugs would return to the kitchen still filled with the porridge. That meant that for a day or two, she and Clifford had something to put in their stomachs.

He was growing fast and she began to worry because he would soon be eight months. His clothes were frayed, and she did her best with the old ones. Once in a while, Emelda would bring in old clothes to be turned into rugs and she would steal one or two and fashion him some crude clothes. But he was a happy baby and the light of her life and never once did she regret taking him as her son.

One morning as she was scrubbing the pots while Clifford sat beside her playing with some pieces of wood she had found in the stable, she heard Emelda calling out to her.

"Barbara, where are you?"

"I'm right here, Mrs. Emelda," she straightened out, groaning inwardly from the strain of bending for a long time. Clifford's teeth were growing, and he bit the pieces of wood, chattering happily.

"Mrs. Sutter needs some things from the attic, and I want you to come up and help me."

"Yes, Ma'am. But please let me finish scrubbing these pots for Mrs. Evans because she needs them for lunch. There's only two more left, Ma'am."

"Very well then. When you're done, come and find me. I'll be in the drawing room."

"Yes, Ma'am."

"Clifford, I want you to be a good boy and stay quietly here in our room. I'm going to help Mrs. Emelda and then I'll be back."

He bounced on his bottom, clapping happily and she sighed. Nancy would have loved her son and she had no doubt that her parents would have adored him too. Clifford was such a beautiful and peaceful child. He never gave her any trouble, even when she left him alone. He would play alone in their room for hours whenever they were busy, not once crying out.

Between taking care of him and the work she did every day, she was too exhausted to do anything other than sleep when she got to bed.

"Here," she gave him a soft biscuit that she had stolen off Mrs. Evans's tray. It would melt in his mouth and there was no risk of him choking on it. "Nibble on this, I'll be back to check on you."

She gave him a loving look and a gentle kiss on his forehead before leaving the room. As she stepped into the forbidden territory as she called the rest of the house on the other side of the kitchen, she wondered. She'd been here for nearly eight months, but barely knew the layout of the house, for she wasn't allowed to go beyond the kitchen door. Being an obedient girl and knowing what was at stake, she refused to give into temptation even when Gladys and Carolyne, Mrs. Evans's daughters tried to get her to go in. She got the feeling that they wanted her to get into trouble and be sent away.

So, when she stepped out of the kitchen and into the hallway, she was confused at first because she had no idea where the drawing room was. The hallway stretched out in both directions, at the end of which was a stairway on one side and a large door on the other. Taking a deep breath and a chance, she walked toward the large door, and the next thing she knew, she was flung to the wall when a man charged out of one of the rooms. He didn't even stop to find out if she was hurt or to even say sorry, and she fumed, wondering who the man was who lacked proper manners. Or maybe he knew she was just a maid and didn't deserve to be treated fairly. Whatever the case, she felt ill treated, but swallowed her ire and went in search of the housekeeper. She heard raised voices coming from the room the man had just exited.

"Oliver should have the money," a woman's shrill voice was saying and she recognized it as that of the mistress of the house. "You always deny him when he asks you for money, and he's your son and heir."

"I have a daughter too and that son and heir as you refer to him, is the bane of my existence, Maryanne. That boy is lazy and good-for-nothing. He won't lift a finger to do anything other than gamble and chase after every skirt in the county including merry widows. My greatest fear is leaving my hard-earned wealth to him. He'll just run through it and ruin the estate. I might as well just leave everything to Penelope."

"You never give him the chance to prove himself."

Realizing that she could get into trouble for eavesdropping if caught, she quickly moved down the corridor and sighed with relief when she saw Emelda emerge from a door down the hall.

"Quick," the woman didn't even give her the chance to catch her breath but grabbed her hand and pulled her along. "The last thing we want is those two seeing us. I hate being drawn into their numerous family disputes."

She practically ran down the hallway in the opposite direction and up the stairway to the attic, Barbara hard on her heels.

"The woman wants me to find the doilies that her mother-in-law used when she once entertained some member of the royal family nearly ten years ago." Emelda's face had a deep scowl, "And all this madness is because some baroness will be visiting us in a few days' time."

Barbara was intrigued by the happenings in the household.

"Start checking in these trunks," Emelda pointed at five large trunks as she walked to the other side of the attic to the small window and opened it, letting in more light. "And be quick about it because I don't like it in here."

Barbara worked swiftly and found what the housekeeper sought. "Mrs. Emelda, could these be what you're looking for?" She held up one of the doilies, a pure white one.

"You're a wonderful girl," Emelda smiled at her. "And now to reward you for your hard work, I want you to pick a few things for your son from this trunk. This woman will never have any more children but refuses to give these away to the poor. Be quick and hide them under your clothes. When I get time again, I'll bring you up here to get some more."

Barbara grabbed as many as she could and stuffed them under her clothes. Then she helped the housekeeper carry the doilies and other tablecloths out of the attic.

"Let me have those," Emelda said, holding out her hands for what Barbara was carrying. "Go back to the kitchen and attend to your son."

"Yes, Ma'am and thank you very much." But even as she went back to the kitchen, she was puzzled at Emelda's sudden kindness. The woman was usually very stern and strict with her and barely spared her any glances. And yet out of nowhere, she'd given her enough good clothes for Clifford. They were of good quality and she would keep them for when they were going to church or travelling somewhere.

Well, she wasn't going to look a gift horse in the mouth and went to her room to put them away, finding that her son had played himself to sleep.

"Oh my darling," she knelt down on the mattress and kissed his soft cheek. "One day, we'll have a nice large bed and all the good things you deserve. But for today, Mrs. Emelda was kind enough to give me some things," and she pulled them from under her clothes, folded them neatly and placed them in the battered carpetbag that she hid under her mattress.

17

TELL ME NO LIES

Barbara was bent over scrubbing a large pot when she felt the uncomfortable sensation of being watched. Clifford was dozing off at his usual spot in the corner of the kitchen and she quickly turned to find a man standing in the doorway leading to the rest of the house. She recognized him as the man who had crashed into her just two days before, and her lips tightened, especially when she noticed that he was looking at her with an evil leer.

"Sir, may I assist you in any way?"

Even though she was angry at how he had treated her, she forced herself to be polite to him. After all, he was the son and heir of her master, Oliver Sutter. Until a few days ago, she'd only heard about him because he was away from home a lot and their paths never crossed.

Oliver rubbed his chin and licked his lips. He was handsome but there was something in his eyes that put her off him and she just wished he would leave. "Well, perhaps you can. I need hot water for my bath, and I want you to bring it up to me in my bedchamber. See that you do so immediately," and saying so, he turned on his heel and left.

"The nerve of the man," Barbara was seething inside. Just who did he think he was, she fumed. Never had she come across such a rude and arrogant man before and she wasn't going to bow to his whims. Besides, that was the work of Gladys or Carolyn and she wasn't going to interfere lest she get a scolding she didn't deserve. She needed this job and wasn't going to cross Mrs. Emelda in any way, not after the kindness she had showed her a few days ago.

Instead, after cleaning the kitchen, she picked her son up and went to her small room. She had two hours to herself each day during which she lay on her straw bed and pondered her future and that of her son.

Clifford's first birthday was coming soon, and she was reminded about her friend. If only she had insisted on finding out the name of the man who had sired Clifford, she would have ventured to take the little boy to his father.

"Well Clifford," she murmured to the sleeping child, "I will steal a piece of cake for you from the master's table for your birthday," she made the promise to her son. Footsteps came down the servants' hallway and stopped outside her door. Someone knocked, "Who is it?"

The person didn't answer but turned the knob and pushed open the door and stepped in. It was Oliver and the look on his face frightened her. This was the dull hour as Mrs. Evans called it; the time when all the servants had time to themselves.

Since they had all received their wages just that morning, her colleagues had all gone to the village square and wouldn't be back for some time, so she was all alone on this side of the house.

She slipped her hand under her pillow then got up from her mattress and moved as far away as she could from him. "Sir, you shouldn't be here," she held her right hand behind her. "This isn't the place for you to be."

"You're just a mere servant and this whole house belongs to me so I can go wherever I please," he looked at the sleeping child, a sneer on his face. "It's interesting to note that you have a child, yet you look at me with those big eyes of yours as if you're innocent."

"Please leave my room," she felt all the anger from before beginning to rise up.

"I will do as I please," he licked his lips. "Stop being prudish when we both know what you want."

"I'm afraid I don't understand you, Sir."

"You're nothing but a pretender. I know your kind and how you give yourself to louts who leave you with children. Were you hoping to come here and ensnare me with your beauty?'

"I didn't ask you to come to my room," her anger was beginning to boil over. Just minutes ago, she'd been thinking about the man who had sired Clifford and how he had turned his back on her friend. Now Nancy was dead, and she was raising this little boy on her own. Now this arrogant man comes into her room and makes false accusations about her. "I came here to work and don't want or need any trouble."

Oliver just laughed her to scorn. "So you say, but your body is ripe for a man, and I mean to enjoy the pleasures you will give me."

"Please leave now," her voice had dropped, which should have warned him had he known her better. But because he didn't, he locked the door and advanced towards her.

"I think not. The kitchen and backyard are empty. I happen to know that your colleagues all went to the village square, so it's just you and me."

He took another step closer and Barbara felt like a cornered cat, so she flew at him, screeching with all her might. The small knife she kept under her pillow for protection was in the hand she'd been hiding behind her back. "I warned you to leave me alone, but you refused to do so and kept coming at me. I came here to work and wasn't looking for trouble, but you just won't leave me alone," she made a swipe at him, but he ducked just in time, and the knife flew out of her hand. Because he hadn't been expecting her to attack him, he took a hasty step backwards and knocked his head against the wall, then fell forward on her straw mattress. Knowing that if he got up, he might hurt her and the baby, she jumped on his back and began pummelling him with fast blows on his head. He raised his hands to cover the back of his head, but she was like one possessed, screaming with all her might.

The splintering door and her son's frightened wails brought her back to her senses and she looked down at the man lying on the mattress. Clifford crawled toward her, and she picked him up and then moved to the furthest corner of the small room and sank down on her knees. She was trembling at the realization of what she had nearly done to the man. Nancy's words came to her, and she remembered what her friend had told her when she had fought with a girl who was trying to bully her.

"You've got to keep your temper in check, Barbara. If you let yourself go, you may one day harm someone or even yourself because of anger. Rage is a terrible thing and like the nuns are always telling us, better is a man who can control his spirit than one who can take a city."

"This woman is mad," Oliver scrambled to his feet when he saw his mother. "I want her gone from here." She could see pieces of straw sticking out of his hair and she knew that his head would be sore for days.

Mrs. Maryanne Sutter stared at Barbara with so much hatred in her eyes. "Who do you think you are?"

"Mama, don't waste your time talking to this worthless girl."

"Don't worry, Son," Maryanne said. "I know your kind," she once again turned to Barbara. "You came into this house hoping to ensnare my son so he would provide for you and your baseborn child. Your wicked plans didn't work, and I want you gone from her before this day ends."

The woman took her son's hand and led him away, murmuring soothing words to him. Emelda came into the room and gave her a pitying look. "What did you do, Barbara?'

"That man is lying against me. I've never spoken to him and it was only two days ago that I even knew who he was. He came into my room when I was resting and I asked him in a polite way to leave, but he refused."

"Well," Emelda sighed, "You heard the woman. You're going to have to leave because she can be a nasty person when she feels that her son has been threatened in any way. Oliver is the light of her life and this will land you in jail if you refuse to go."

Barbara nodded, "I understand," she said. "Thank you for all that you've done for me these past few months."

"Pack up your bags and go and hide in the stables while I go and appease Mrs. Sutter and her son. Once the coast is clear, Roger the stableman will drive you to the town square so you can take the train or stagecoach out of here."

"Thank you, Ma'am."

~

Roger let her down a few miles from the house. "Are you sure you'll be all right?" He looked concerned.

"Yes, thank you," she stepped off the cart and picked her son and bag up. She didn't want him to tell her former employer where he had dropped her off just in case he was pressed to do so. She knew that a man like Oliver could be vindictive and try to find out where she had gone just to cause her more trouble. She looked around her and even though she was a little frightened of what the future held, still, this was in the middle of nowhere and she would disappear in the farmlands. Perhaps some family would offer her a job and a place to stay for a few days while she thought about what to do. Or maybe, she could find work as a dairy maid and work outside the house. "You've been so kind to me, thank you."

She waited for Roger to turn the cart around and return to the Sutters' estate before she strapped her son on her back, picked up her bag, and slipped into a path on the side that didn't look like it was used much.

After a few yards, Clifford began wriggling on her back, and she put him down. Since he was now walking, even though he wasn't quite one year old, he didn't like being carried so much anymore. "We'll get there, my son," she said as she took his hand and they resumed their journey, even though she had no idea where *there* was.

DRIFTING AWAY

Smoke rising up lazily to the sky in the distance alerted Barbara to the fact that they were getting close to a dwelling. They had been walking for close to three hours and she was thankful that before Emelda sent her away, the woman had given her a large piece of pie, a chunk of fruit cake and milk in a bottle.

"I always feared that this would happen," she told Barbara as she slipped a guinea into her hand. "That was the reason I never let you get out of the kitchen. But that foolish boy clearly recognized that you were new in the household and wanted to try and do to you what Gladys and Carolyn freely allow him to do to them." Emelda smiled, "I'm proud of you, and when I see my sister, I'll tell her that you're a good girl."

"Thank you, Mrs. Emelda," she'd said with tears in her eyes. Never again would she jump to conclusions about a person. Emelda had really surprised her.

Autumn was drawing closer, and the weather was changing fast. She didn't want to get caught up in the rain because of her son.

"Mama," Clifford said, and Barbara looked down at him. She thought he might be needing something from her.

"Yes, my son?"

He grinned up at her and pointed in the distance. "House," was all he said because his vocabulary was limited. "House," he repeated.

"Why yes. What a clever boy you are! That's indeed a house, and the smoke indicates that there are people at home." Seeing how tired he looked, she strapped him onto her back and picked up their bag. "Let's go and seek shelter from whoever is in that house."

But as her steps took her closer, she began to fear what might be waiting for them in that home. What if it was another man and he attacked her? Or more than one man?

The wailing was getting too much for Larry to bear. He'd never seen a woman bringing forth a child nor even an animal foaling or calving. Mr. Graham only reared geldings and so the chance of taking care of a pregnant animal had never risen. Yet he was the only one at home when Mrs. Helen Graham, the mistress of the house went into labour. His master, Mr. Joseph Graham had travelled to London to take care of business.

Since Larry was their only employee, he'd been instructed to keep the home safe. He was terrified of anything going wrong with his mistress and he wished someone would hear the screams and come to his assistance. But their house was miles away from any other. The Grahams lived in isolation and whereas Larry had found it suitable at first, in times like this he was a disadvantage. He couldn't even leave the woman alone to go to the nearest neighbour's place and ask for help.

"Dear Lord, please send me help," he murmured.

Mrs. Graham was frightened because this was her first child and she had no idea of what to expect. In the year or so that he'd been working for the Grahams, he'd noticed that they didn't seem to have any friends at all. No one came calling, and they never went out as a couple to visit anyone in the vicinity. They didn't even attend service at the small church about a mile down the road. The only person who ever left home was Mr. Graham when he was going on one of his journeys to London. Larry had never even seen a midwife coming this way to check on Mrs. Graham to ensure that she and the baby were alright.

"Dear Lord, please help me," he whispered again as he made his way to the well behind the house to fetch some more water. He had no idea why he felt that it was important for him to boil water, plenty of it, but he followed his instincts.

As he was returning to the house carrying a pail in each hand, he chanced to look toward the path leading up to the gate and saw a woman walking on the path toward the compound. She'd also seen him, and he stopped to stare for a moment. Hope filled his heart when she reached the gate, and putting down the pails, he rushed forward to open it and let her in. He was sure that as a woman, she would know what to do for his mistress.

"Good day, Sir," Barbara was exhausted from the long walk and carrying Clifford. "My son and I seek a place to bed for the night."

"You have a son?" Larry blinked twice. He'd been dazzled by her beauty and initially hadn't noticed the child strapped to her back.

"Yes," Barbara turned slightly so the man could see her son, "His name is Clifford. We've been walking a long way."

"You're indeed a sight for sore eyes," he said and noted the cautious look in her eyes. "My name is Lawrence Trent and I work on this farm. My mistress is in the house and is about to have a baby." And as if to confirm his words, a loud wail came from the house. "It's Mrs. Graham's first child and she is as scared as I am. We both don't know what to do."

"Quick," Barbara took charge without a second thought. She dropped the bag and unstrapped Clifford from her back, handing him over to Larry. "Would you hold him while I check on your mistress? Those wails are frightening, and we have to make sure that she's alright. Is there any hot water in the house?"

"Yes, Ma'am," Larry held the child close and picked up the bag Barbara had dropped and followed her, feeling quite relieved that someone else had taken charge. When he entered the house, she was already headed for the room where the wailing was coming from.

"Wait," he called out, "Mrs. Graham might be frightened to see a stranger so let me introduce you."

"Okay then, shall we go in?"

Larry nodded and knocked on the bedroom door. "Mrs. Graham, I brought someone here to help you." But the woman didn't respond, and they concluded that she was asleep, so they went back into the living room.

"Clifford is usually very fussy around strangers, but I'm surprised that he's taken to you so fast."

"He looks hungry, perhaps a glass of warm milk and a piece of pie will endear me to him."

To her surprise, Clifford nodded and slipped his hand into Larry's, leaving her to check on the woman. Immediately she opened the door, a foul stench assailed her nostrils. The curtains were drawn, and the room was dark.

"Mrs. Graham," she approached the bed and the woman's eyes flew open. Forcing herself not to gag, she entered the room.

Barbara was surprised to find that she wasn't much older than her, and as Larry had said, she looked really frightened. "My name is Barbara Coomb and I'm here to help you."

"I just want this pain to stop," she sobbed but no tears came. "Please help me."

"I'll do that right away, but first let me open the windows and curtains and clean up a little bit."

"No," Helen screamed, "Come and pull this thing out of me. It hurts too much."

The screaming woman reminded Barbara a little of Nancy and after opening the windows and letting much-needed fresh air in, she returned to her patient.

"Let me examine you," and she proceeded to do so swiftly, noting that the woman still had some time to go. But she wasn't going to mention that because she didn't want her to panic. "You're doing well and in a short time, you'll be holding your baby." The beddings were all soiled and Barbara brought in the hot water from the other room and cleaned the woman and the room up. In a short while, the air was once again fresh, and once Helen was clean and her clothes changed, she calmed down.

"I'm here to help you, and together, we'll bring this little one into the world in a short time."

"I didn't realize that having a baby is such a painful process," Helen gave a small laugh. She was a pretty young woman with dark, kind eyes. "Mr. Graham, my husband, travelled to London for business but hasn't returned. Poor Larry had to listen to me cursing like one of those sailors at the Liverpool docks," they both giggled but Helen's ended on a long moan.

Barbara made her patient as comfortable as she could, speaking gently to her through every contraction and finally, nearly six hours later, Helen brought forth a beautiful baby girl.

"Here is your sweet baby, all ready to nurse," Barbara placed the clean infant in her mother's arms. The child immediately snuggled at her mother's breast, instinctively reaching for nourishment.

"You truly are a Godsend," Helen looked up from nursing her daughter. "You're so young and yet you really knew what to do to keep me calm. I was panicking especially when I thought that Larry would have to deliver my baby. It's like you've been delivering babies all your life."

Barbara smiled, not wanting to tell the woman that this was just the second baby she'd helped bring into the world. "Let's just say that I have some experience and I'm glad that I was able to help you."

"Your calmness above all is what helped," though Helen was smiling and clearly happy to be holding her baby, Barbara could see that something was troubling her.

"Mrs. Helen, is there something troubling you? Are you still in pain?" The woman shook her head but turned her face away.

"I'm here for you whenever you need me," Barbara prayed that she would be allowed to stay even for a short while.

"Where did you come from?" Helen asked and Barbara knew she was trying to change the subject.

"We travelled from Leighton," Barbara lied. She didn't want Helen to find out that she'd been working for the Sutters who lived on the other side of Cheddington just in case she knew them. So, she made it as if she'd come from much further.

"We? I didn't realize that there was someone else with you," Barbara saw the shutters coming down in her eyes.

"It's my son, his name is Clifford and he's one year old."

"Oh!" Helen's face brightened once more. "Please tell me that you'll stay here. I need all the help I can get."

"Don't you have to first ask your husband for his permission before taking on someone to help you in the house?"

"Mr. Graham travels a lot and he'll be happy that I have someone to help me with the baby. Larry is here, of course, but he's a man and doesn't know what to do to help with a baby." Barbara silently pondered the woman's words. "I'll pay you a reasonable wage, please stay with me."

"But what about the sleeping arrangements? I notice that your house has two bedrooms and you will need one for the baby." Barbara prayed that she wouldn't be asked to sleep in the open kitchen. Were she alone, she might accept that but her son needed a warm place.

"Tell Larry to show you around the house. Just off the kitchen is another room which is empty. It was supposed to be a pantry when Mr. Graham first built this house, but it turned out to be larger than what we had intended it to be and also warmer. So Mr. Graham put in a window and we turned it into a room for our guests. You'll find that it's really cool during summer and warm during winter. There's a bed and even a small chest of drawers for you to store your things in. Please just say yes."

"Thank you, Mrs. Graham, I'll be happy to stay and work for you."

"It's really my pleasure, Barbara," Helen beamed.

"I'm sorry to have kept you hungry. I hope you don't mind that I asked Larry to slaughter a chicken so I could prepare you some broth. I've also made some soft mashed potatoes so you can regain your strength."

"Well, next time ask me before you slaughter any of the chickens."

"Yes, of course," Barbara walked to the door. "Is there anything else you would like to eat?"

"Just get me whatever is there. When I'm back on my feet, we'll talk about the dishes that should be prepared and served."

"Yes, Ma'am."

As Barbara lay on the soft bed, a smile came into her eyes. This was the first comfortable bed she had slept in in ages. The last time she'd had a good bed was at home when her grandmother was still alive, and then for two months at the convent. After that, it had been straw mattresses for her.

Helen Graham was a surprising woman, but Barbara was determined that she would do her best to make her new employer happy. A lot was at stake and as she listened to her son's soft snores in the darkness, she knew that they would be happy here. Her only prayer was that Mr. Graham would turn out to be a good person for she was done dealing with arrogant men.

Which took her mind back to Larry. He was a handsome man, and the shadows in his eyes told a story of their own. He had seemed pleased that they were staying but didn't say anything. She had also noticed that he had strong hands and yet he was really gentle when he held her son. What would they feel like if they were wrapped around her, she wondered, then shook herself from her foolish thoughts. It was such stupidity that had led to this situation where she had a child that she was raising on her own. Nancy had probably wondered the same thing about Clifford's father and then not being content with just thoughts, had acted it out and ended up in a mess.

Even being this far from the convent, she could still hear the Mother Superior's teachings. "The lust of the eyes will soon lead you to the lust of the flesh," she had told them one Sunday morning. "Good girls don't allow themselves to look at anything that will lead them to temptation. Even the Lord Jesus said that if your eyes cause you to sin, it is better to pluck them out and enter heaven as a blind person than have both eyes and perish in the fires of hell."

Hell, Barbara had discovered, wasn't only in the afterlife. Life could also be hell on earth, especially when one was hungry and had no good bed to sleep in. But heaven was also here on earth as she had found out that evening. After having a large plate of mashed potatoes, chicken and green peas, she was going to be quite full.

"Gluttony will lead you to hell," Mother Superior had said on another occasion. "Eat only what is enough for you. The Apostle Paul admonished the Christians in Corinth saying, 'Food for the stomach and the stomach for food, but the Good Lord will destroy them both.'"

Barbara chuckled softly, "I'll be gluttonous for only a little while because good food has been denied us for so long," she murmured sleepily. "But I can't help it."

~

In his room above the stable, Larry wondered who Barbara was and how she had come to them. It wasn't like the Graham Farm was along any usual pathway, if anything, they were tucked away from the normal roads.

He'd seen the love in her eyes for her little boy, but there was sadness also. She was either a widow, a very young one at that or else a man had deceived her and then tossed her aside.

He found himself thinking about her even as he dozed off. When Mrs. Graham had told him to show her to the guest room, he'd felt something like butterflies in his stomach. Though he felt very foolish, he knew that he had fallen in love at first sight with a stranger. Would she allow him to woo her and win her hand, or would she shut him down because of what some man had done to her in the past?

19

BROKEN PIECES

"I could listen to him forever," Barbara said as she watched Clifford toddle across the living room, chattering to Samantha who was listening keenly to him.

"And he's so good for Samantha," Helen agreed. "Because of your son, she is already crawling at only six months. At this rate, she will walk before she turns one."

"Clifford walked at eleven months and I was so happy, for then I didn't have to carry him everywhere."

"He must look like his father because apart from his sweet disposition, none of his other features are like yours." Helen looked at the two children who were playing happily. "My Samantha looks so much like her father."

"She is a beautiful girl, and you should be so proud of her."

"At least I am," Helen turned away and Barbara was troubled. She liked it here because her employers, especially Helen was really kind to her.

And Larry was the best. Just thinking about him made her have funny feelings in her stomach, like many butterflies were fluttering around inside. Then she shook herself out of her reverie. Helen wasn't as happy as she should be, and Barbara thought that it might be because she was missing her husband. Like she had said before, Mr. Graham travelled a lot.

"You must miss Mr. Graham very much when he goes away," Barbara offered. Helen made a sound between a sniff and a snort.

"Let me get the children ready for their dinner," Barbara got the feeling that the woman wanted to be left alone. Helen's mood swings made her really uncomfortable. One minute she would be going on about how much she loved her husband and wished he would stay home more, but in the next, she would be making faces when his name came up. She'd just done the latter and Barbara didn't want to be subjected to a tirade about terrible husbands. Once she was sure the children would be all right as she got them their dinner, she left the living room.

Larry was in the kitchen dressing a chicken when she entered, and he gave her a smile that made her heart flutter. "Can it be that you grow more beautiful each day?" He asked in his deep voice that he had lowered so Helen wouldn't hear what he was saying. "Seeing you smile is like feeling the rays of the sun on my face, gently kissing it on a beautiful spring morning." He finished what he was doing and moved away from the sink.

"Larry," her face turned bright red and he shook his head as he walked to the door.

"Barbara, it's true that when I see you smile, all I want to do is find the man who hurt you and tear his face off," the smile was gone from his face and eyes and he walked out of the kitchen through the backdoor and she sighed. He needed to know the truth about Clifford.

~

"Barbara, you amaze me," Larry told her later that evening when they were seated on the kitchen porch. "You gave up so much for your friend. I really respect and admire your loyalty to your friendship. Not many people would do that, especially not when they know that there will be a lot of pain and suffering ahead."

"Nancy was always there for me when my own family wasn't," she smiled sadly. "The people I believed to be my parents, sent me off to a convent school because they knew my grandmother was dying. She was the only one who really loved and cared for me. Sending me away to boarding school was their way of getting rid of me but at the time, I didn't know it. For two years, I was angry with Grandma Edna because I thought she had abandoned me. But Nancy shared everything she had with me. When other people looked down on me because of my lowly status, Nancy was there for me and defended me."

"Did she ever tell you who the father of her baby was?" Larry took her hand and linked their fingers together.

"No, but it doesn't matter anymore. Clifford is my son and I love him so much. I would do the same thing all over again even after going through what I have since he was born."

"Everyone sees just how much the little boy loves you."

"He has grown really attached to you," Barbara told him. They sat holding hands for a while, listening to the night sounds as darkness fell.

"Larry, may I ask you something?" She spoke softly just in case anyone came up and heard them. She didn't want her employers to overhear their conversation.

"Sure, go ahead."

She moved out of his embrace, stood up and walked a few steps away. Under the soft porch lantern, she turned to him. "Do you get the feeling that Helen is unhappy?"

"What makes you say that?" he also got up and came to stand closer to her.

"Her mood swings. One minute she's happy and the next, she is all angry. I'm afraid to be around her for fear of offending her."

Larry sighed. He'd noticed that his employers didn't have the perfect marriage that they wanted everyone to believe they had. In the past, he'd come upon Helen weeping in the kitchen, but she always said it was because of the onions she was chopping up.

"I've been with them a year longer than you, but I thought the same thing. But then Helen got pregnant and they seemed to be so happy. Mr. Graham stopped travelling so much for a while, and he paid a lot of attention to her. Actually, at the time you arrived here, that was the first time he'd been gone in months."

"I would have thought that his wife and child would keep him close and happy, but it seems like all he does is travel."

"He is a successful businessman and besides, whenever he travels, he brings back such beautiful gifts for Helen."

Barbara sighed, "It's not always about gifts, Larry. A woman needs to feel her husband's love and the only way to do that is for him to be with her."

Larry turned to Barbara, "What about you, Barbara?"

"What about me," she asked him, a slight frown on her face, "What do you mean?"

"Given a husband who travels a lot and brings you back beautiful gifts, and a man who has very little but loves you with all his heart, who would you choose?"

She didn't hesitate with her answer, "The man who loves me and is always close by unless something urgent comes up is the man I would most certainly choose. Money can't buy love or bring comfort. Love is what counts for me."

Her answer pleased him, and he found himself grinning.

"Why do you look so happy?"

"Nothing," he said.

20
BROKEN TRUST

"**I** love you so much, Barbara," Larry whispered, taking her left hand and sliding a ring on her fourth finger. "This ring isn't much; I got it for two pence at the fair, but one day I'll adorn you with gold, diamonds, and other precious stones."

"Oh Larry, you silly man," Barbara was laughing and crying at the same time, "I don't need all those things to be happy. I just want your heart, that's all that matters to me."

"And you have my heart, my beautiful girl, all of it, now and forever," he smiled down at her. "My mother made me promise to marry a queen."

"I don't understand," Barbara was surprised at his comment because in all the time she'd known him, he never talked about his family. She didn't even know that his mother was still alive. "You've never talked about your family before," she said and saw his face pale. "I'm sorry if it's a sensitive topic for you."

"My family is a topic I never discuss with anyone," he said and saw her face fall. "Not you, my love," he hastened to add.

"It's just that I haven't thought about them in a long while and so talking about them just never comes up."

"I understand."

"No, you don't," he took her hand again. "My father, mother, and four siblings all died in prison. Of course, not at the same time but in the short span of six years, I lost all six members of my family."

"I'm so sorry, Larry. I didn't know."

"You couldn't have because it's something I don't like to share. But my father nearly killed a man he stole from when I was thirteen. Mr. Alistair Bramble had taken me in to help the family, but my father came by his house one day and pretended to be ill. When he was allowed to stay the night, he sneaked out of the room, and Mr. Alistair caught him stealing from him." Larry was deeply ashamed, and he prayed that Barbara wouldn't turn away from him in disgust for his father's actions. "Papa attacked Mr. Alistair, leaving him for dead and made away with nearly two thousand pounds. But he was arrested, and we lost our home, so we had to go to prison with him. I've always wondered why he wasn't taken to Newgate, but in the end, it didn't matter. Prison is prison and I lost my whole family. Since we didn't have any money to pay for better quarters, we were put in one of the terrible sections of Fleet Street Prison and the conditions in there were appalling." He looked down. "My sisters and brothers died one after the other from cholera, dysentery, and typhoid and then my father followed. He left my mother and me, but she also left me."

"If your father was the one who'd done wrong, why weren't you pardoned after his death?"

"It usually doesn't work like that, my darling. Mr. Alistair or in this case, his sister Miss Matilda felt that we had to pay for my father's crimes, so Mama and I were still imprisoned." He didn't like thinking about that part of his life. "But two years later, I received a pardon from Mr. Alistair. Apparently, the letter I wrote him begging for his forgiveness was hidden in his desk behind some other files and documents and he found it much later, and that's when he acted." He twisted his lips, "It was too late for my family."

Barbara didn't know what to say to comfort the man she loved, and so all she did was rub his hand gently.

"But let's not dwell on sadness, because we now have each other," he raised her chin. "My mother used to tell me that I should never marry just any woman. She said that the woman I fell in love with should be the queen of my heart, nothing short of that."

"She sounds like quite a remarkable woman."

"She was and I know she would have loved you."

"Are you saying I'm a queen?"

He nodded, "You're the queen of my heart, Barbara. You sit in my heart and reign in it with love. You're the last person I think about before I sleep and the first one when I wake up. I want to be there for you and Clifford more than anything in the world." He touched the ring that he'd just slipped onto her finger, "I did this the wrong way," and saying that, he went down on one knee. "Barbara Dorcas Coomb, would you marry me?"

"Yes, yes," she cried happily. "Please don't kneel."

"I do it because I respect and honour you and promise that I will love you forever."

"Oh Larry, I'm so happy."

~

She was still smiling as she walked back to the house to check on Clifford who she'd left sleeping. The kitchen door was well oiled, so it barely made a sound as she opened it and slipped in. Her son was still asleep in their bedroom and she looked down at him, a gentle smile on her face.

At two and a half years, his features were quite distinct, and she always felt that if she ever came face to face with the man who had sired him, she would recognize him. Clifford's hair was carrot red and curly, and he had deep green eyes. But he also had Nancy's beautiful smile and sweet disposition.

"Oh Nancy," she murmured, twisting the ring on her finger. "I wish you had waited before giving yourself to that horrid man who rejected you when you needed him most."

She'd seen Cookie's daughter and Nancy mistreated and abandoned by men they had trusted with their virtue. It wasn't going to happen to her, at least not willingly. But even if a man ever tried to take her virtue away by force, she would fight with all her might until the very end.

Her love for Larry was growing stronger with each passing day because never had he even once made her feel like she had to defend her honour. He treated her like a lady, with respect.

It was time to prepare the evening meal and she left Clifford still sleeping and walked back into the kitchen, stopping short when she found Helen weeping at the sink.

"Mrs. Graham, is Samantha alright?" Her first concern was always the child. "What has happened?"

"Nothing," Helen dashed the tears away with the back of her hand and left the kitchen hurriedly. Barbara was getting more and more perplexed by the day. Mr. Graham was home and to all intents and purposes, his wife should have been happy. But Helen was miserable, and Barbara was glad that when the master was at home, she and her son ate in the kitchen. Larry would sometimes join them, but Helen preferred that he took his meals in his room above the stables.

When dinner was over and Barbara went to clear up the table, she found the food untouched. Her employers were in their bedroom and their bedroom door was slightly ajar so she could hear their conversation.

"You can go back to your mistress," Helen was sobbing. "Why did you even come home if you don't want to be here?"

"Would you keep your voice down? Do you want the world to hear you? Then allow me to open the windows wide so that you can tell the whole world our problems."

"Let them hear and know that my husband is a fraud. You lie that you love me, but you have many mistresses and don't care about us. Go back to them and don't bother coming back home."

"I can't reason with you when you're like this."

Barbara fled before Mr. Graham came out of their bedroom and found her eavesdropping. But she went to bed quite troubled.

21

BROKEN HEARTS

Larry noticed that Barbara was staying away from him and didn't seem as happy as before. She kept herself busy in the house all the time, and whenever he entered a room, she would excuse herself and leave in a hurry. This went on for a few days before he decided that enough was enough.

"Barbara," he ran after her one day when she and Clifford were walking back home from church. "Why do I get the feeling that you've been avoiding me these past few days? Have I done something to offend you? Did I do something wrong?"

Barbara stopped and twisted her lips as she turned to him. It was true that she'd been avoiding him because her feelings were all mixed up. When she had first come to this household a year and a half ago, she'd thought that Mr. and Mrs. Graham had the perfect marriage despite the fact that he was fifteen years her senior. Yet now it seemed that their marriage had deep cracks in it and all they had been doing is covering up their marital problems. What did that mean for her and Larry? It was clear that Helen was getting more and more agitated with each passing day. But then was it fair taking out her fears on Larry?

"I've just been very busy in the house," she finally said, releasing Clifford who was wriggling in an attempt to get away from her. He went over to Larry, who hoisted him onto his broad shoulders. Not for the first time, Barbara thought he would make a good father. He always made time for Clifford, no matter how busy he was.

"To me it's not about you being busy but more of avoiding me. I feel like I may have wronged you in some way. Whatever I did, please let me know how I can make things right."

"It's not you," she sighed. "Things have been so tense in the house. Mr. Graham said he was minimizing his business trips so he could stay home with his wife and child and I expected that his presence at home would make Mrs. Graham happy. But she's so miserable and agitated all the time. They fight into the late hours of the night, and I'm getting quite concerned about what this means for us."

"Once or twice, I've heard them, and it bothers me too. But maybe it's because I've been here longer than you and have seen this same thing happening. After Mrs. Graham found out that she was expecting a child, the fighting stopped. But what does their fighting have to do with us?'

"I know that they'd been married for about five years and when I first came here, I thought they were the perfect couple. Now it seems like all they do is quarrel. Is there any hope for us?'

Larry could see the genuine concern in her eyes. "Barbara, no matter what anyone tells you, there's no such thing as a perfect husband or a perfect wife, or even a perfect marriage. We're all in this race called life and trying to live as best as we can. But I believe that two people can work through their differences and problems and build a good and strong marriage. It's all about knowing what's at stake should the marriage fail and working hard to ensure that that doesn't happen."

Larry's words made a lot of sense, but she was still afraid. "What can we do to help them?"

He shook his head, "Some fights are private and only meant for the parties concerned. Let's pray for them that they will soon find their way. Now, I know that you still have two hours before you have to go back home and prepare dinner. How about I take you and Clifford to the town square for a walk?"

"I have to get him home and feed him."

"We'll have lunch at one of the inns. I know Clifford loves pie and broth."

She gave him a dazzling smile and he felt his heart melting inside. This woman was so beautiful and yet loved the simple things in life. How had he been so blessed?

"We'd like that very much," and they walked to the town square chattering happily. Clifford rode on Larry's shoulders and he greeted everyone who passed by. Barbara thought she heard one or two people commenting that they made a beautiful family.

The Victoria Inn beckoned, and as soon as they stepped through its colourful doors, a short, plump woman welcomed them. "Look at the three of you," she beamed at them. "Such a perfect little family. Do come in out of the cold. Autumn will soon be here, and the winds are mighty harsh this time of the year."

"We'd just like a quick bite before heading home," Larry said. "Those delicious pies that you make are what brought us here."

"You're in luck because I just turned out a fresh batch a few minutes ago."

They were soon seated in the parlour and enjoying their meal. Apart from the three of them, there were two other people partaking of different dishes. It was clear that at this time of the day, the inn wasn't all that busy but from the other aromas wafting into the parlour from the kitchen, a lot of food was being prepared.

"I'm surprised that there aren't many people here. This woman makes such delicious dishes and should have many customers," Barbara said as she bit into another pie and savoured the delicious taste. "These are really good."

"Well, they probably left for London or elsewhere while the weather is still good. But also, people these days travel more by train down to London because they are safer than the stagecoaches which are always targeted by highwaymen."

"It would be sad to see such a quaint little place shut down for lack of customers."

"There's no chance of that happening because one or two stagecoaches still pass this way."

"You're right," she watched Larry as he paid attention to Clifford, cutting his pie into small, bite-size pieces. "But when I finally have my own store, I'll make sure that no one works on Sunday, not even myself. It's the Lord's Day and people need to rest."

"Minimal work isn't bad because people still have to eat," he waved a hand. "Like us for example, if Mrs. Victoria didn't open this place on Sundays then we wouldn't be here enjoying this pie and chicken broth. You would have had to go back home and prepare food for us when you're tired."

"Well, I hope Mrs. Victoria also gets enough time to rest."

"She probably does on the days when business is slow," there was the sudden rumbling of thunder in the distance. "I need to get both of you back home where it is warm. Looks like the rain might come down at any time."

Barbara ensured that Clifford was done eating while Larry when to settle their bill. He returned with a small package which he handed over to her. "Mrs. Victoria said this is a piece of fruitcake for our son," he chuckled softly as he picked the boy up and once more hoisted him on his shoulders. "Shall we head home then?"

"Let me just thank Mrs. Victoria," Barbara slipped through the door leading to the kitchen and found their hostess, thanked her and followed Larry out of the inn.

None of them wanted the day to end but the threat of rain made them hurry back. They just made it back to the house before the skies opened up and the rain came down hard.

"I have to check on the animals," Larry said when he had brought them to the kitchen door. They stood at the bottom of the porch steps, not wanting to leave each other.

"Thank you for today. We had a really wonderful time."

"It's always my pleasure," he reached out a hand and touched her cheek. Then he noticed the kitchen curtain move and felt slightly uncomfortable. Someone was watching them, and it made him very uneasy. He wasn't sure whether it was Helen or her husband but thought it better not to mention it to Barbara.

"Go in now, and make sure you both stay very warm."

22

PERFECT STRANGERS

Christmas that year was a quiet affair and it seemed like it was only the children who enjoyed it. Helen spent her time locked up in her bedroom, and Mr. Graham disappeared off to somewhere.

When the children were taking their afternoon nap, Barbara sneaked out of the house and went to find Larry. He was rubbing down one of the four horses in the stable. "You look upset, or should I say troubled?"

"That's because I am," she entered the stable and leaned against one of the stalls. A big black horse came up to her and nuzzled her shoulder. "Camper, you're a good boy," she rubbed his nose then turned to Larry. "I wish there were something I could do for Mr. and Mrs. Graham. It's Christmas but there's not a single decoration in place, nothing special. It's just like a normal day, and only the children enjoyed the day. Christmas shouldn't be like this."

"Barbara, you've got to understand that our employers are going through a difficult time in their marriage and that happens to all couples," he touched the tip of her nose. "You and I will have similar moments when things won't be going so well for us. When that happens, it won't mean that we don't love each other then, but it will be an opportunity for us to grow together. This is an opportunity for our employers to find out how to deal with their personal issues and not make it about ourselves."

"I wasn't making this about myself," she mumbled.

"I didn't mean it like that," he smiled at her. "What I mean is that I also love Christmas and promised that I would celebrate every one of them when I was finally free from prison. But I also understand that Christmas is all about our Saviour Jesus and not pomp and glory. With or without decorations, Christmas can still be beautiful when we remember why we celebrate the holiday at all."

She smiled sheepishly, "I guess you're right. It's just that when I was growing up, Grandma Edna would make a big deal of it. We would have a large tree and decorate it from the twentieth of December. Then there would be gifts and candy all over the place, she made such a big deal of everything that I got used to doing things in that way. Last year, we all had such a wonderful time here that I thought this year would be the same."

"We're alive and that's all that matters."

"I know," she smiled him. "Let me go back into the house and prepare dinner. Thank you for reminding me of what's important."

∽

Spring gave way to summer, and Barbara was relieved when Mr. Graham announced that he was going away on another business trip. Things were really strained between the couple and they no longer hid their animosity toward each other. It also made her very uncomfortable when the two of them used her to pass on messages to each other even though they were under the same roof.

Barbara also noticed that Helen's countenance had changed toward her. The woman was no longer as friendly toward her as before. She and Larry were so happy, and it seemed like the more Barbara's life was going so well, the angrier her employer got.

"I should leave," she sobbed to Larry one evening when Helen had been particularly hasty to her. "Nothing I do seems to please Mrs. Graham. She shouted at Clifford, and I held onto my anger by a whisker."

"Barbara, calm down," Larry took her in his arms.

"So, this is what you spend all your time doing instead of working," Helen's shrill voice caused them to spring apart guiltily. "You already have a child with a man who abandoned you, yet here you are throwing yourself at another. What if he gets you in the family way, are you sure he can even take care of you?"

"I'm sorry," Barbara said.

"I'll not have the two of your carrying on right under my roof. This isn't a brothel where you can do whatever you want. Now, go into the house and you," she pointed at Larry, "From today, I don't want you anywhere near Barbara. Or I'll kick you both out on your ears."

"It won't happen again, Ma'am," Larry promised.

"You better make sure it doesn't," and giving them a final glare, she walked away.

"Don't say a word in haste and anger," Larry warned in a low voice when Barbara opened her mouth. "She is going through a lot of pain and has no one to talk to and so she acts out."

Barbara wasn't feeling benevolent toward her employer at that particular moment so she merely snorted and made her way back to the house.

Helen was in the kitchen when Barbara entered, and she turned. "I'm sorry Barbara, it wasn't kind of me to speak to you like that. It's just that all this is too much for me," she covered her face with her palms.

"Mrs. Graham, is there anything I can do to help?" Barbara's anger faded away when she saw her employer's distress.

"I'm pregnant again," Helen blurted out and then started weeping. "Mr. Graham wants a boy and I don't know what I'll do if this is another girl."

"Ma'am," Barbara gently took her hand and led her to the living room and helped her sit on the couch. "You shouldn't be distressing yourself in this condition. I'm sure Mr. Graham will be happy when you and the baby are fine."

Helen shook her head, "You don't know my husband," she said. "He wanted a boy the first time around and was so disappointed. That's why he pays no attention to Samantha. He says that if I can't have a boy for him this time, he'll take a mistress who will give him a son. He needs a son and heir to take over his estate."

Barbara felt so angry at her employer for his insensitive handling of his wife. How dare he distress his wife—and in her condition at that? She had come to the realization that men were very selfish and only cared about their needs. Would Larry one day change and begin to place unrealistic demands on her? What if he did that when they were married? Would she stand for it and bear it like this poor woman was doing?

"What am I going to do?" Helen moaned.

"Mrs. Graham, please calm down. There's enough time for your husband to change his mind. Stop fighting with him and say calm even when you feel like shouting or arguing with him."

"He makes it so hard for me to be calm. I know that he has a mistress in London even though he denies it."

"What if he's telling you the truth? You might be agitating yourself for nothing when he is innocent." Barbara longed to believe in her own words but found it hard. She had noticed Mr. Graham giving her some funny looks whenever he thought she wasn't looking, and it made her really uncomfortable. Many times, she'd wanted to share her fears with Larry, but she didn't want her fiancé getting angry and doing something rash in his anger.

But she was glad when the weeping woman finally took herself to her bedroom.

It was a tough seven months for the household, and especially for Helen. As her due date drew closer, she got even more agitated.

"You need a good midwife," Barbara told her. "This baby will need a lot of care and I may not provide it all alone."

"I'll send for Mrs. Hopkins, the village midwife, to come in and help you. Remind me later," Helen said.

Jane Hopkins was a no-nonsense woman who, when called in, told Helen that she had to stop fretting so much. "You need all your energy to bring this baby into the world and all that whimpering won't do you any good."

Barbara was glad the middle-aged woman was present because her toughness made Helen calm down.

In the last week of Helen's pregnancy, she decided to stay at the house just in case the baby came at night and Larry couldn't get to her house in time to call her.

"I'm really afraid for this woman," she whispered to Barbara when they were in the kitchen boiling water when Helen went into labour.

"But why? I thought she was doing so well. Your presence here has calmed her down and I believe she'll have this baby without any problems at all."

Jane shook her head, "Mrs. Graham is too distressed, and I fear that if this baby is a girl, she will go out of her mind."

23

LETTING GO

"**M**rs. Graham," Jane hesitated, casting a fearful glance at Barbara who was cleaning up after the delivery.

"Is it a boy?" Helen raised herself on her elbows. "Is it a boy?"

Jane shook her head, "Ma'am, you have a beautiful daughter."

Helen gave a sharp cry and collapsed back against the pillows. Jane passed the infant to Barbara and rushed to attend to her. Her examination was frantic, and she turned a white face to Barbara.

"Quick, get Mr. Graham. Ask him to send for a doctor."

The doctor, when he came nearly an hour later, pronounced Helen Graham dead and Barbara wanted to fly at Mr. Graham and scream at him that it was all his fault. He had pushed his wife into desperation and when she didn't get when she wanted, she gave up on life. The shock of not presenting her husband with his much-desired son and heir was too much for her to handle.

Helen was buried a day after her death, and those who came to condole with the family commented on how much her husband had loved her. Barbara listened to all that while seething inwardly with rage.

Taking care of a new-born baby who had no mother was not much trouble because Mr. Graham paid one of the village women to be her wet nurse. He disappeared to London soon after, and Barbara felt relieved that he had gone.

"I think I should start thinking about leaving," Barbara told Larry one morning two weeks after Helen's burial. "Every time I look at little Penelope, I get so angry. This man drove his wife to her death."

"Barbara, you don't know that."

"If he hadn't kept telling her to make sure she had a baby boy, the poor woman would have enjoyed her pregnancy and not been agitated all the time. Mrs. Hopkins told me that Helen probably died of a broken heart."

"She's not a physician and you should be careful about listening to village gossip." Barbara glared at him and walked back to the house to carry on with her chores.

Larry watched her walking away and sighed. He too was worried about all that had happened in the past few days. His master was getting harsher with him. At first, he'd put it down to the fact that the man was mourning the loss of his young wife. But then on two occasions, Larry had caught him watching Barbara in a way that troubled him. Perhaps she was right, maybe it was time they both left.

They could go and begin a new life away from here. He didn't have much, but he was sure that they would make it in London.

But before he could ask her to leave with him, his employer returned and terminated his services just out of the blue.

"You're a lazy, good-for-nothing man," Mr. Graham told him. "You have cost me losses, and that means that I'll have to take your wages to cover them."

Barbara was in tears as she bid Larry farewell. "Come with me, my love," he begged her. "I don't have much, actually I don't have anything because Mr. Graham withheld my wages for the past two months, but I know we can make something of our lives in London."

"Larry, this man refused to give you your wages and what I have isn't much. Helen promised me good wages, but when I asked her about it, she said she was feeding me and my son, and I should be glad that she'd taken us in. If we come with you, we'll only hold you back. Go ahead and prepare for us and when you're ready, you can send for us and we'll come to you."

"I hate leaving you here because I feel that I don't trust Mr. Graham."

"Don't worry, I can take care of myself. Besides, the man is hardly ever at home and also, Sam and Penny need me for now."

"I promise that as soon as I get my first wages, I'll get a house in a good place and then send for you and Clifford."

She smiled through her tears, "We'll be counting the days until we can come to you, Larry. Now, go with God," she said as the train's whistle went off.

"Will you wait for me, my Darling?" Larry tried to hide his fears.

"I promise to come to you as a virtuous wife, Larry. I have made my promise to you and I pray that you do the same."

"With all my heart," he said, and she believed him.

They shared their first kiss before the train's whistle made them both jump. Larry also kissed Clifford who'd been silently watching them as if understanding whatever was going on. Then he left.

With Larry gone, Barbara became more cautious and especially when Mr. Graham was around. He employed a couple to stay at the house. Linda Grey was the housekeeper or so she claimed while her husband was the stableman and also took care of the grounds around the house.

Even though Linda was a lazy woman, Barbara tolerated her presence in the house because then Mr. Graham kept his distance.

"You're a young and beautiful woman," Linda told her one evening, "And a very foolish one too."

"Why would you say that?"

"Here is a wealthy man who is a widower and very eligible," the woman winked at her. "If I were you, I would fall into his arms and insist on his marrying me."

"What?"

"The man is obviously attracted to you and you're wasting your life pining for a man who is probably cavorting with all the harlots of London and has forgotten all about you."

"Mrs. Grey, thank you for the advice," Barbara was sad. Three months had passed but Larry hadn't written a single letter to tell her how he was doing or even sending for them. Could Linda be right? Had Larry forgotten all about them?

"Just think about it. What's to stop you from indulging yourself? Helen Graham left a lot of jewellery which can be yours if you play your cards right."

24

NOT EVERYTHING IS AS IT SEEMS

So, this was what London looks like, Barbara thought as she stepped off the train and helped her son down.

"Your bag, Miss," one of the porters tossed her battered carpetbag onto the platform. There were people running all over the place, and it was frightening. Someone shoved her and she wanted to turn and shout at them, but her son tagged at her dress.

"Mama," four-year-old Clifford slipped his hand into hers, "I don't like it here. This place smells bad."

"Neither do I like it, my love, but what can we do?"

"Why did we leave Sam and Penny? We should have stayed with them."

Barbara twisted her lips as she picked up all their worldly possessions. "We had to leave because," she was spared answering when someone shouted, and they had to move out of the way in a hurry. "Let's go and find somewhere to stay," she told her son even though she had no idea where they were going.

On the train, she'd listened to people as they talked about workhouses where poor people could find work to do and a place to live. She needed that so much, now that she had nothing.

From what Larry had told her when they were back on the farm, workhouses were terrible places which took advantage of helpless people. But it was certainly better than having no work or place to live.

They walked out of the station and joined the throng of people, and she found herself standing beside a park. Spotting an empty bench, she led her son to it and then sank down tiredly on it.

People were hurrying in all directions and barely spared her a glance. At least, Clifford wasn't hungry yet because she'd fed him an hour before the train pulled up into Euston Station. She had no money to even find lodging for her and Clifford.

Mr. Graham had tossed her out of his house and his words stung terribly. "You came here looking like a scruffy stray dog and we offered you a home. I'm trying to make a decent woman of you, yet your kind never changes. Instead of agreeing to be my wife, you want to go and play the harlot with all the louts in this village. I have no need of you anymore."

Without money or anything, he'd told her to leave before he brought in the village constable to drag her out of his house. She'd hidden in the stables until she saw him leave the house then slipped back in and rummaged through the drawers in his bedroom and found some money. She only took what she thought was due to her, hoping to find enough to convey them to London.

But because of the rains, their journey was slow and hard. By the time they got to London, she barely had any money left.

Clifford climbed onto her lap and curled up, immediately falling asleep.

"Dear God, please help me," she closed her eyes wearily. She sensed someone standing in front of her and immediately thought of the tens of thieves and pickpockets lurking around every corner of London. Her arms tightened around her son and she opened her eyes, ready to confront any threat.

"Larry?" She whispered when she saw the man standing in front of her.

"I couldn't believe my eyes when I saw you seated here on this bench," he said, his eyes didn't seem friendly at all. "Where is your husband, are you here with him?"

"My husband?" She was puzzled at his reaction. "You were supposed to send for us so we could get married. What are you talking about?"

"Don't lie to me, Barbara. Or did the glittering gold turn into dust?"

"Larry, we came here to find you, why are you being so unkind to us?"

"Because dear girl, you can no longer fool me with your innocent looking eyes. I wondered why you refused to leave that farm with me but now I know why."

Barbara bowed her head to look at her sleeping child, tears prickling behind her eyelids. She had envisioned a totally different kind of reception when she finally found Larry.

"You promised to send for us. We waited a whole year, but you never came back."

"And why would I have returned for you when you already belonged to another? All the promises we made to each other were lies."

"Larry, I never lied to you."

"I wrote to you one month after I left and even sent you money for fare so you would come to me. Instead, it was your husband who replied and told me not to bother you again because you were now a married woman, and happily, he added."

"Mr. Graham?" Barbara got a sinking feeling in the pit of her stomach.

"Who else? So, you decided that the widower's money was good enough," Larry snarled and saw the hurt in her eyes. Something wasn't right, but he was too angry to think straight.

"I never got married to Mr. Graham or anyone else. All I was doing was helping him take care of his new baby daughter and Sam," she told him in a quiet voice. "It hurts me that you would think I would do something like that after the promises we made to each other." She pulled the ring off her finger, "I have no more need of this," she held it out to him.

"I'm sorry, but after I got the letter, I met someone else. Her name is Catherine, and her father is a merchant who owns ships and has taken me into the business. One day, it will all belong to me."

"Good for you," Barbara refused to let him see her cry. No man was worth her tears. She and Clifford would be fine.

"You can't sit here," Larry said.

"What do you care? Go back to your wealthy heiress and her merchant father. Clifford and I will be fine."

"Barbara , , ,"

"Just go," and saying that, she turned away from him.

"Here is some money, and there are workhouses in Whitechapel that will take you in."

Larry stood there waiting for her to accept the money, but she kept her back turned to him. He placed the money on the bench next to her and then with one final look of regret, he left her sitting on the bench. His last image of her was her pale face.

PART III
THE GOLDEN AGE

25
EXPECTING THE UNEXPECTED

"**W**ere you a good boy for Mrs. Maple?" Barbara bent down to kiss her son's cheek. The woman she was referring to was the one who minded her little boy when she was out working at the yarn factory. "I hope you didn't give Mrs. Maple a hard time, Clifford."

"Mama, Mrs. Maple sleeps all the time," Clifford's small face was screwed into a scowl. "And I'm hungry. She forgot to give me any lunch."

Barbara struggled not to get angry for she had no one else she could leave her son with when she went to work. Mrs. Maple was the only one who was willing to take on the task of minding a four-year-old boy, even though her rate was really high. But at least it enabled Barbara to go to work and make money so she could be independent.

The house, or rather rooms, she lived in were small but decent and were just a stone's throw away from where she worked. They were part of a larger terraced house the landlord had converted into rooms and rented out to people who had families. The house Barbara and Clifford lived in had four other tenants who also worked at the yarn factory with her. She never stopped thanking God for enabling her get the job and then the accommodation, even though it was wanting in so many ways. The tenants shared a common kitchen, but no one stored their food there for fear of it being stolen.

"Come, let's find something to eat," she looked into one of the tins in the second room which she used as a kitchen and living room. She hoped to find a cookie that would assuage her son's hunger until she could prepare something for their dinner, but the tin was empty. The only food she found in her rooms was a bowl of oatmeal. At least she would be getting her wages in two days' time and she would replenish their food supplies. "Clifford, all we have is some oatmeal. I'll just heat a little water and make us some oatmeal porridge. What do you say?"

"Yes, Mama," he grinned at her. She loved this little boy who never complained even when life was so tough. She refused to think about Larry, who was probably a married man by now. It hurt, but each day she forced herself to think about her future and Clifford's and not dwell on what could never be.

Paddington Yarn Factory, the place where she worked, had undergone vast changes since she came to work here four months ago. A fire had nearly razed one of the warehouses to the ground, but mercifully, no one was injured. Ownership had since changed hands and even though there was some slight adjustment to the wages, Barbara often felt like her purse had large holes through which her money dropped and disappeared.

Paying for her house and Mrs. Maple to watch Clifford meant that she barely had anything left for food. So, on

Sunday afternoons when she and Clifford left church, she would pass by the Farmer's Market in Whitechapel and head for the bins where waste was dumped. She would take whatever she found, scrape off the rotten side and carry the good parts home for their weekly food. It was a degrading life, but she always told herself that she was lucky to be alive and working, and also living in a place that though considered a slum, was much better than others she'd seen.

Not for the first time, she felt guilty for ever having considered abandoning her sweet son at an orphanage just so she could get into the first workhouse Larry had sent her to. The foreman there had told her that they were hiring but their living quarters didn't provide a place for children to stay. It was either find an orphanage and leave her son there or miss out on the job.

Dejected and desperate, Barbara had considered doing that when she ran into Mrs. Maple. The woman had also come to the workhouse hoping to get employed but they said she was too old and slow. That's when they got talking and Mrs. Maple told Barbara about the yarn factory.

"Because I can't work in the factory, why don't I mind your child for you, and you can pay me?"

They agreed on a figure which Mrs. Maple changed twice. Because she was desperate and liked working at the factory, Barbara simply gave in and watched her money getting less and less with each passing month.

She cried herself to sleep on days when she found herself thinking about what her life might have been with Larry. Larry! The name that brought her so much pain! Why couldn't she forget all about him? There were a few nice-looking young men who showed an interest in her, and then there were also the not-so-nice ones. She ignored all of them because she didn't think they deserved a single moment of her attention.

Each time she met a man, the first thing she would tell him was that she had a son, and then watched as their countenance fell. Clearly, no man wanted to raise another man's child, and she used that as an excuse not to allow anyone to get close to her.

"Mama, is there more?" Clifford licked the cup with his tongue and then used his finger to scoop out the remaining porridge. Barbara wanted to weep when she saw her son's still hungry face. What kind of a mother was she, who couldn't even feed her own child?

There was a knock at her door, and she opened it, surprised to find Mrs. Maple standing there. "Good evening, please do come in."

"Well," the older woman looked at Clifford who had come to stand next to his mother. "I wasn't feeling very well and may have forgotten to give the boy his lunch," she pushed a hot package into Barbara's hands and turned and hurriedly walked away.

"Mama, what is it?'

"Dinner," Barbara closed the door and set the package on their makeshift table. She unwrapped it and the aroma of fried fish and chips filled their small house, causing her stomach to growl. "Come and eat," she told her son and he needed no second bidding.

Barbara took a few bites just to quieten her rumbling stomach, but she left most of it for her son. A growing boy needs much food, she thought, and she had already started thinking about finding a better job even though she knew it would be very hard. Whenever she got the chance, she would peruse through the newspapers to find out who were hiring for better wages. The only problem was that most employers didn't allow the incumbents to have families or children. She wanted more for her son than growing up in the small rooms of a terraced house in a slum.

"Thank you, Mama," he wiped his oily hands on his shirt, and she flinched.

"Come here," she told him. "What did I tell you about wiping your fingers on your clothes?"

"Rats will eat me."

"Yes. Now let me take these clothes off so you can prepare for bed."

The farm hadn't changed much, and Larry stood at the gate wondering if he was doing the right thing or not. Maybe he shouldn't have come here to disrupt Barbara's life, especially not after the way he had treated her when he saw her in London six months ago. But he had to see her one last time and ask for her forgiveness. It hurt him to think that she might now be Mr. Graham's new wife.

As he was just standing there, he saw Mr. Graham emerge from the front door of his house holding a pregnant woman by the small of her back. The two children he remembered followed them out of the house, but the adults simply ignored them. What gave him joy, however, was when he looked closely at the pregnant woman. It wasn't Barbara.

"What do you want?" Mr. Graham looked slightly uncomfortable when their eyes met. Larry no longer feared the man who had been his employer.

"Over a year ago, I wrote to Barbara and even sent her money to come to me in London. You knew we were courting and yet you didn't pass the letter to her. Instead, you wrote and told me not to bother her since she was your wife," Larry said and had the satisfaction of seeing the woman at Mr. Graham's side stiffen. She looked like someone who didn't stand for nonsense.

"Who is Barbara?" she asked in a deep commanding voice. Mr. Graham turned pale. "Joseph, I asked you who Barbara is."

"Some inconsequential person," Mr. Graham said. "She really doesn't matter anymore."

Larry was having none of that and he was angry that Mr. Graham could so easily and carelessly dismiss Barbara. "Barbara is the young woman who took care of this man's children for three years. But he tossed her out mercilessly. That's the kind of man your husband is, Ma'am."

"Is this true, Joseph? That you kicked that poor woman out of your house? Why?"

"My love, it wasn't like that at all," his eyes were pleading with Larry not to say anything more that would cause damage to his marriage. Much as Larry wanted to hurt the man who had been so cruel to both Barbara and him, he remembered that as a Christian, the Bible forbade him from taking revenge. So, he sighed and decided to let the matter rest. What right did he have to destroy the man's marriage? He was the one who had stupidly believed Mr. Graham and rejected Barbara, letting her down. Now he had no idea where she was or even whether she was safe or not.

"Never mind," he said. "Ma'am, I'm sorry," and he turned and walked away, leaving them arguing. Or rather it was the new

Mrs. Graham who was scolding her husband while he pleaded with her.

Like all the other men in her life, Larry had let Barbara down and he felt lower than a heel. Where could she be? He'd searched for her in all the workhouses in Whitechapel, but he hadn't found her, and that was why he had decided to travel to Cheddington. The love of his life had vanished, as if she'd just dropped off the surface of the earth.

"Oh Barbara," he groaned as he boarded the train that would take him back to London. "Where are you, my love?"

BEAUTY THROUGH PAIN

The warehouse was buzzing with excitement and Barbara was soon to find out why.

"Mr. Paddington will be visiting the factory," one of the ladies who worked with her said. Elise Milligan was her agemate but Barbara avoided making friends with any of her colleagues. For one, they looked down on her because she was new, and they also despised her for having a child out of wedlock. She also didn't have any spare time to go on any of their excursions around London because of Clifford.

"Who is Mr. Paddington?" She asked, then felt foolish for doing so. "Of course, he's the owner of the factory."

"Yes, he's coming to inspect this place for the first time since buying it, and we're all expected to be on our best behaviour."

Barbara had barely settled down at her workstation when her supervisor came and stood at her large spindle.

"You're slow again," Bernard Castor told her, but she was keeping pace with the large machine that had intimidated her the first time she came here. She was in charge of ensuring that all the bobbins were well wound up with yarn and that required a lot of concentration.

"Mr. Castor, please," she whispered.

"There's a woman standing outside at the gate braying for you."

"Who is she?" Barbara couldn't imagine who might be coming to see her at the factory.

"She's the woman who takes care of your child."

"Oh!" Barbara slowed the loom and then stood up.

"Did I say you could leave the machine?"

There were snickers around her which she ignored. Mrs. Maple never bothered her at work unless there was an emergency. The last one was when Clifford had fallen and sprained his wrist about a month ago.

"My son must be ill," she said as she put her apron away and rushed to the side door and then outside. She didn't realize that Bernard was behind her until she got to the gate.

"Clifford, my Love, what's the problem?" She held out her hands and he practically jumped into them and nuzzled her neck. "Mrs. Maple?"

"The Little One has been restless since you left, and he kept crying for you."

"Clifford, what's wrong?"

"Mama," he wrapped his little arms around her neck and held on tight. At least he didn't have a high temperature and for that, she was thankful.

"Miss Coomb, you need to get back in right now. You're holding up the production queue."

"My love, Mrs. Maple will take you to the store so you can get some candy," that got his attention and he released her.

"The one with many colours?"

She laughed, "Yes, any kind you want." She put her hand in her pocket and pulled out two pennies which she handed over to Mrs. Maple. Clifford finally let go.

She was still smiling when she took her place in the assembly line.

"You think you're special," Bernard hissed at her. "You've just lucky the manager didn't find you away from your work station. The next time you do something like that, I'll fire you on the spot because I don't want you to cost me my job."

Barbara chose to ignore him and went back to work, bending her head and ignoring the chatter that was going on around her, intermingled with the whirling sounds of the looms as they spun and twisted the yarn.

But then suddenly all noise ceased. At first, Barbara thought everyone had decided to be quiet as they worked, but the silence was pulsing with something like excitement.

"And this here is our twisting section where yarn is rolled onto bobbins," Roland McGuire, the factory's Irish Manager was telling someone. Barbara had only seen the man from afar because he never came into the warehouse, leaving the supervisors to take care of the workers.

"How many bobbins do you make per day?" a deep voice asked.

"Right now, we're doing close to ten thousand spools per day, Sir."

"That sounds reasonable, though I need to go through the books to see what is going on."

"Yes, Sir," they came closer to Barbara's station and when she saw the new owner, her heart skipped a beat. He looked exactly like how her four-year-old son would look like in about twenty-five years, right down to the carrot red hair and green eyes. Then she blinked, turning away so she wouldn't be caught staring at him.

"Mr. Clifford Paddington is the new owner of this factory and I'm showing him around so he can see what goes on around here and meet the workers," Ronald introduced the floor supervisors to their new owner but Barbara was still struck at how much her son looked like the man who was walking around the warehouse floor.

Clifford? The man even shared a name with her son, what was going on?

She heard a buzz as the owner and manager moved away and then noticed that the other ladies were giving her funny looks.

"I always knew there was something odd about you," Bernard scorned. He had told her to stay behind when her shift ended. "It has now become clear to me why you carry yourself around with such airs, as if you were related to Queen Victoria."

"I don't know what you mean," she was genuinely puzzled. "I need to go home to my son."

"Yes, the son you had with Mr. Clifford Paddington. I asked and found out that your son's name is also Clifford."

"You heard me calling him that, but I don't know what you mean by what you're saying."

"It is rumoured that Mrs. Paddington is one very tough woman and she doesn't stand for nonsense," Bernard drew closer, a lewd look on his face. "If she finds out that you've been cavorting with her husband, there's no telling what she might do to you. For one, you'll lose your job and then your home and next thing, you'll be languishing on the streets of London."

"There's nothing going on between me and Mr. Paddington and there has never been."

"Then how do you explain the fact that your son looks so much like him and they even share a name?"

"That's just a coincidence."

He shook his head, "The way I see it, you have only one choice," he licked his lips. "You know that I can provide for you and even put you on some extra shifts so you can make more money."

Barbara looked at him distastefully, but she also didn't want to lose her job and her home. Besides, this job enabled her to keep her son close by, and losing it wasn't an option.

"You can be my woman and I'll take very good care of you," he reached out a hand to touch her head, but she slapped it away.

"Get away from me," she hissed, her eyes blazing at him.

His expression became ugly, "So you think you're too good for me? We'll see about that. I'm going to send Mrs. Paddington a note and she will come here to meet the harlot who is breaking up her home."

"You do your worst," Barbara told him. "But one day, you'll get what's coming to you. You can go ahead and fire me or tell people whatever you want to. My dignity is not for sale to anyone, not even for a job. I'm going home to see my son."

~

Clifford Paddington took off his jacket and coat and hung them on the rack in the hallway. Hurried footsteps came towards him and he smiled.

"My love, you look so beautiful today."

"The woman who walked toward him narrowed her eyes at him. "Clifford, what have you gone and done this time?"

He laughed shortly, "My darling, you know how much I love you," he held out his arms to his wife. She just took his breath away and he always thanked the Lord for blessing him with this sweet woman.

"That I do," she walked into his arms. "Now, tell me what's on your mind."

He sighed and held her by the shoulders at arms' length. "I visited the factory today."

"You always visit the factory, isn't that why you bought it in the first place?"

"Yes, but I've never had the chance to walk on the floor and see firsthand how the work is done."

"What happened?"

"The manager told me about a young woman and her child. They say the child is mine, but you know that I've never once looked at another woman."

"Then why would someone come up with such a terrible rumour?"

"To embarrass me," Clifford said. "There is a lot of underlying resentment toward me because I bought the factory and have begun making a lot of changes. The old guard aren't too keen on the changes I'm making around the factory and I wouldn't be surprised if one of them started the rumour."

"What is the name of the woman?"

"I don't know. Is that important?"

She gave him an indecipherable look and shook her head. "No, it doesn't matter," then she turned away so he wouldn't see the curious gleam that had entered her eyes.

I GIVE YOU ALL I HAVE

Barbara couldn't believe what was happening in her life. Suddenly, out of the blue, Mrs. Maple declared that she wasn't cut out to take care of a small, boisterous boy like Clifford.

"Why today of all days, Mrs. Maple?" Barbara was nearly in tears. "Why didn't you tell me this so I could find someone else to take care of my son?"

The woman just shrugged, and her shifty eyes and nervous twitching of her lips made Barbara realise that something else was going on.

"Has someone paid you to frustrate me?" She asked, narrowing her eyes at the woman.

"I don't know what you mean," Mrs. Maple's sallow skin turned a bright red and Barbara had her answer.

She knew who was behind her woes and her lips tightened. "Anyway, thank you for helping me out these past few months. You can come for your wages in two days' time when I get my pay."

"I'm truly sorry about this, Miss Coomb," the woman shuffled out and Barbara sighed. What was she going to do? It was the factory's busiest time as they were trying to fill as many orders as possible before winter fully set in. She couldn't afford to miss work, not for a single minute but she also couldn't leave her son alone at home.

"Well, Clifford," she bent down. "Get onto my back. You and I have some business to take care of," she knew this would mean the end of her job, but she was tired of being pushed around by a bully.

The moment she set foot in the factory, Bernard was waiting for her. He came over, grinning like the cat that had licked the cream. He was rubbing his hands gleefully and there was blatant malice in his eyes.

"You're going to get it today," he told her. "I sent Mrs. Paddington a little anonymous note telling her that there was some floozy claiming to have borne a son for her husband," he giggled wickedly.

"I know you were the one who paid off Mrs. Maple so she wouldn't take care of my son. You want me fired and I'll go but just know this," she said softly, "One day, it will be your turn to leave this place and believe me, it won't be amicable. You've frustrated so many others like me and it's just a matter of time for you."

He sneered at her, "That's the least of your worries at the moment. The manager wants to see you in his office at once."

"Let me put my bag . . ."

"Oh no," he steered her away from her workstation. "I don't think you'll be staying after your meeting," he winked, and she glared at him. "Quick, don't keep the manager waiting."

And saying that, he led her up one flight of stairs and opened the manager's office door, practically pushed her inside, and then followed her in. She could hear him snickering behind her.

Barbara was surprised to find a woman in the office. Her back was turned to them and she seemed to be searching for something on the shelves.

"Mrs. Paddington, here is the woman," the way Bernard said it made Barbara's heart sink.

"Right," the woman said, and Barbara felt chills running down her back. Then she turned and they came face to face, each staring at the other in shock.

Then they both moved and screamed as they ran into each other's arms. Barbara even forgot that Clifford was still strapped on her back.

"Nancy!"

"Barbara!"

They made so much noise that Clifford started crying. Hurried footsteps sounded on the corridor outside and the door was flung open.

"Nancy my love, are you alright?" Clifford Paddington was immediately at his wife's side.

"Darling," she moved into his embrace and for a moment was too overcome to speak. Barbara tried to calm Clifford down as much as she could. She got a piece of candy from her pocket and gave it to him. She wanted to pinch herself to be sure that she wasn't dreaming. Nancy, her best friend, was alive and she was here.

"Darling," Nancy tried again, "This is Barbara, the woman I told you about, the one who helped me when I was back at the convent."

"Does she work here?'

"Yes, and this," she pointed at Clifford, who hid his neck in Barbara's neck, "Is our son, Clifford. The child everyone was saying is yours and they were right because he is."

"You named him for me?" The man's hushed tones made Barbara realise that he was also in shock.

"Yes. Barbara took him away after I gave birth," she turned to Barbara. "After I left the convent, I went to your home, but I was told that you no longer belonged with them."

Barbara smiled sadly, "It's a long story."

"Which we want to hear, but not here at the factory," she looked at her husband who nodded. "We shall all go home at once and I don't care where you live. Barbara, you and Clifford are coming to live with us."

The older Clifford laughed, "My love, aren't you forgetting something?"

"What?" Nancy demanded.

"Barbara might be married. How will you explain to her husband that you want her to live with us?"

"Are you married?" Nancy turned her eyes to Barbara. She fleetingly thought of Larry but then pushed him to the back of her mind. He no longer belonged in her life and didn't deserve a second thought.

"No."

"Engaged or betrothed?"

"None of those things," she said.

"That's settled then," Nancy said. "Will my son come to me?" She looked nervous and uncertain and Barbara's heart went out to her.

"He'll soon warm up to you, have no fear."

28
FIGHTING LOVE

"And that's the sum of our lives till this morning," Barbara finished telling her story later that afternoon. The older Clifford had his son in his arms and the little boy was gazing at his father with wonderment.

"Mama?"

"Yes?" two voices said simultaneously.

"Force of habit, I'm sorry," Barbara giggled nervously.

"Don't be," Nancy took her hand. "You've been the only mother my little Clifford has known since he was born and we'll never take that away from you," she wiped her eyes. "You gave up so much for me and I don't know how I'll ever repay you. Because of you, my son is alive and here with us."

"We can never thank you enough," Clifford Senior added his voice to his wife's. "Nancy always told me that you were an exceptional woman and I now truly believe it."

Barbara wanted to know more about what had happened to her friend and how she got reconciled to the father of her child, so she asked her.

"After I left home, I went to your place but found the burials had been done," she said in a quiet voice. "I was told you had died just after your parents and I was devastated. How is it that you're still alive?"

Nancy sighed and threw a glance at her husband, who nodded silently. "After you left, I went to the infirmary because my stomach was killing me. That's where the Mother Superior found me and gave me the news of my parents' deaths. The woman was so cold and detached and didn't even wait to see how I'd taken the news," her face hardened. "I'm glad she was recalled to Rome after that fire. By the time I left the convent, it was confirmed that she wouldn't be coming back. Apparently, Rome found out how she was mistreating orphans and the destitute girls instead of taking care of them. All the donations people used to give, were never used for their intended purposes and instead, Sister Mary Claire diverted the funds for other uses."

"Darling, you're straying," Clifford said gently.

"I'm sorry," Nancy laughed. "Well, I collapsed and lay on the floor for a long while since the infirmary was empty. That was the time the fire broke out in our dormitory and everyone was rushing around screaming and wailing. There was so much confusion for days and no one came to the infirmary. It was one of the kitchen women who was coming to check on something in the infirmary that found me. She put me to bed and then called for help. Twenty girls died in that fire and for many days, everyone thought I was among the dead."

"Oh Nancy, how did they get it so wrong?"

"Some girl got into my bed on the night we were in the shed as I was getting Clifford. When her body was found, they thought it was me."

They sat in silence for a while, each lost in their own thoughts.

"It was nearly seven days before the kitchen woman found me. I nearly died because I was bleeding, and no one had attended to me because of all the confusion."

Clifford picked the story up, "After Nancy's parents died, we received news that she had also perished in the fire at school. I refused to believe that the woman I loved was dead. It hit me that I had been a fool to abandon her and I rushed to school after the burial to find out more information. I wasn't satisfied about the fire and wanted to get more explanation, so I went there," he shook his head. "I knew that one of the people buried was Nancy, but I just couldn't accept it. So, when I got to St. Agatha's, I insisted on hearing what had started the fire. In the process, someone realised that Nancy was still alive and told me about it."

"He asked me to marry him, but I was too distraught and just wanted to go home and confirm that my parents were really dead."

"So, they buried someone else in your place? Did they have to exhume the body?"

Nancy shook her head. "After doing a head count and checking the records, it was discovered that the girl was one of the orphans at the convent. Her name was Irene Mason."

"I knew Irene," Barbara lowered her head.

"All they did was change the headstone to read her name because she had no family who would have claimed her body."

184

"Why didn't your housekeeper tell you where I was? I went to find your parents and after burying them, Mrs. Florence was the one who took me to Cheddington to work with her sister. I was there for nearly a year."

"At the time we got home, all the servants had been paid off and left. So, I eventually forgave Clifford and he helped me manage my parents' estate as well as sell the house. Then we came to London," she took Barbara's hand once again. "But I never stopped searching for you and hoping that you would one day find me."

Much later as Clifford was down in the cot that had been moved to Barbara's room for the time being, she sat on the small balcony and listened to the night sounds. This was like a dream and she was so happy for her friend. The family was reunited, and she already felt like an outsider.

Nancy had showed her the room that she'd always kept ready for her son. In it was everything that Clifford needed.

"As soon as we came to London and bought this house, I started preparing the nursery. With each passing year, I refused to believe that I would never see my son or you again. So, I bought clothes progressively at par with his perceived growth."

Barbara knew that Nancy and her husband meant well but she would eventually have to leave. She couldn't imagine her life without Clifford, but he wasn't hers to keep. It would be painful to let go and leave him behind, but it was the only thing to do. It was her desire to see him well settled in his father's household that kept her here.

He was a confused and frightened little boy, and the last thing she wanted to do was hurt him in any way. There was a soft knock; then the door knob turned. It was Nancy.

"I was hoping you weren't yet asleep," she came to the balcony. "It's really chilly out here."

"I got lost in my thoughts."

"Barbara, even though you smile and look cheerful, there's pain in your eyes. Is it because of your family?"

29

ALL I WANT IS YOU

This was the worst street of London for a hungry and starving man to walk along. The aroma of fish and chips mingled with candy and pies had Larry's stomach growling loudly, startling a woman who was passing by him.

His life was a big mess and he felt that he deserved it. Catherine and her father were very unforgiving, and he was lucky he wasn't behind bars for his actions. They'd called him a fraudster like his father and though it hurt, he felt that it wasn't far from the truth.

Mr. Fontaine, Catherine's father was enraged to see his daughter quite inconsolable when Larry told her that he couldn't marry her because his heart belonged to someone else.

"Make sure our paths never meet or so help me, I'll make you rue the day you were born," had been his parting words to Larry. They kicked him out of the living quarters without anything save the shirt on his back. He had begged to be allowed to take his clothes and purse, but he was threatened with prison.

All his savings for a year and a half were gone, locked up in that room where the rest of his belongings were.

All he had in his pocket were two pennies. At least they would buy him a stick of candy which he could chew on to assuage the hunger pangs.

Edna's Candy Store was across the street and he made his way there. The name sounded familiar, but he couldn't quite place it. He pushed open the door and walked up to the counter.

Barbara thought she was dreaming when the door chimes announced another customer. She looked up, a ready smile on her face and it froze when she saw who it was. He looked weary and dishevelled. It was mid morning, and there was a lull in customers, and in the other room, she was boiling some sugar syrup for a fresh batch of boiled sweets. The children especially loved her candy because they got a handful for a penny.

"Larry," she managed to say at last and he looked up, shocked to find her standing behind the counter.

"Barbara?" He looked around, "Where is Clifford."

"A friend is caring for him as I work," even though her anger at him returned, she was touched that he remembered to ask about the little boy who was at home with his mother. Nancy and Clifford were getting along very well, and with each passing day, Barbara distanced herself so he would settle down. And his father doted on him, treating him like a precious jewel.

Because of their gratitude, they had asked her what she wanted them to do for her and she told them of her dream of owning and opening a candy store. No expense was spared to set her up in this delightful little store and she loved being in charge. But all that was hidden from the man who was standing before her.

"You work here now? I didn't know that, and I pass here frequently."

"Well, yes, I work here now," she indicated her apron. "I was in the back room boiling some sugar syrup to make more candy for the children. Did you need anything?" She thought about his cruelty to her six months ago and her lips tightened. "I'm surprised your wife let you come out this far to the low-end parts of London." She was being mean, and she knew it.

He shook his head, "Catherine and I never got married," he saw the surprise on her face and gave her a lopsided smile. "I can never marry anyone."

"Why not?"

"Because I'm still in love with you, Barbara. Do you know that I even went back to Cheddington, to Mr. Graham's farm to look for you?"

"Oh!"

"I thought you might have gone back after I so cruelly abandoned you."

"I thought about it, but," she shrugged. It was true that she'd been tempted to return but thinking about how the man had deceived Larry and kept her in the dark for a whole year made her realise that she could never trust him. Besides that, his cruel insensitivity had led to the death of his first wife and she didn't think she could bear him being her husband.

"I'm so sorry, Barbara," he swayed from hunger.

"Sit before you collapse," she told him quickly, pointing at the small bench in the store. "Have you eaten anything all day?"

He shook his head.

Barbara went into the next room and returned with a tin and a bottle of milk. "There's a sandwich and a piece of pie in the tin."

Larry needed no second bidding but greedily devoured the simple meal. But Barbara refused to feel sorry for him.

"I have nothing, Barbara," he wiped his lips with the back of his hand. "I've lost everything, but the pain is nothing compared to the thought that I lost you because of my own foolishness."

"Does this mean you're looking for work?"

He nodded, "Anything to enable me to get back on my feet again." He looked around, "Are you hiring?"

"We need someone, but I have to ask the owner first. Na . . . Mrs. Paddington owns this store. Why don't you come back tomorrow? I'll speak with her and see what she has to say."

"Thank you," he rose to his feet feeling stronger now that he'd received nourishment. "This is a quaint and pretty place, much like what you and I used to talk about."

"Would you like a tour of the place? There are only two rooms, this one and the one where I make all the candy. Come this way," she let him precede her into the back room and saw the surprise on his face. She laughed a little, "Yes, Mrs. Paddington bought all this equipment so this candy store can be the best. Right now, we're not producing as much as we should because I can't operate some of those machines and that's why we need someone. If Mrs.

Paddington is agreeable, you can help me make the candy like you used to back at the Graham Farm."

"I'd like that very much," he said, pulling out the two pennies from his pocket. "What can I get for these?"

"There's always something for everyone, no matter how much money a person has," she smiled.

"Thank you for the tour, but I must be leaving now," he had to find a place to sleep before it got dark. They went back to the front room. "Barbara, I really love you," he said and left.

"Are you sure it's the right thing to do, Barbara?" Nancy looked concerned. "That man broke your heart."

"I never stopped loving him, Nancy. Even though my mind wanted to see him suffer for what he put me through, my heart broke when I saw the despair in his eyes."

"Well, what do you want me to do?"

"I told him you own the store and he is looking for work. Back when we were on Mr. Graham's farm, I taught him how to make sweets. We would spend hours talking about how we would one day have our own candy store."

"Do you think this man still loves you?"

Barbara nodded, "I saw it in his eyes and heard it in his voice. He told me so. He broke off his engagement with a wealthy woman and even went back to the farm in Cheddington to look for me."

"Well, I forgave Clifford even after what he'd done to me. The heart wants what it wants and can't be denied. I'll come to the store tomorrow and meet with this young man who has you in knots. But if I get the feeling that Larry will break your heart again, I'll send him packing so fast that he won't have time to say a word."

Barbara hugged her friend, "And I would have it no other way. I'm so glad you're on my side."

"You've been through enough pain and for as long as I live, I'll never let anyone hurt you again. This is your golden era now and it's the time for you to finally enjoy your life."

30
ALWAYS AND FOREVER

Birds sang and waves crashed along the shore. Larry held out a hand to Barbara and she placed hers in it. He pulled her close into a bone-crushing grasp, but she only felt happiness, closing her eyes against his chest. He had brought her to the shores of the Thames River for the day because he had something special to ask her. She had a rough idea about what it was but held her peace. This was his time and she wasn't going to deny him the opportunity.

He buried his face against her neck and whispered words she couldn't hear, but her heart knew what he was saying.

He let her go and cupped her face in his strong calloused hands. He raised her face and looked deeply into her eyes.

"I love you so much, Barbara. I adore you with every fibre of my being," his voice was shaky, and she placed a hand on his chest, feeling the steady beating of his heart.

"Oh Larry, I love you too."

He closed his eyes and groaned softly. "I don't deserve you, not after what I did."

Her eyes softened, "No, you don't," she whispered and smiled cheekily when his eyelids shot up in alarm. Seeing the lopsided grin on her face, he swallowed.

"You're a little imp, Barbara. My heart nearly stopped."

"Larry," her voice was serious. "You broke my heart but I'm glad it happened. That made me stronger and kept me from opening my heart to anyone else ever again."

"I really hurt you, and for the rest of my life, I'm going to work hard in every way to make myself worthy of you, because I love you so much."

Barbara pulled away, seeing the pain in his eyes. "Do you really mean that?" She badly wanted to believe him but the pain in her heart was still fresh.

"Barbara," he took her hand. There were lines of strain about his lip as he said, "Do you love me enough to give me your heart and trust that I will never break it again?"

It was like the whole universe was silently listening and waiting for her response. Even the waves seemed to be still at that moment.

She took a deep breath, "I want to be free," she said at last and his hands fell away.

"Free from me?" He asked hoarsely, running a shaking hand through his hair.

She shook her head and saw hope flare up once again in his eyes. "Only your true love can set me free, Larry. Your promise is what I long for more than anything else."

His hands trembled as he drew her close once again. He held her gently and tenderly and she felt like crying. "Barbara, my darling, your love is my beacon in the darkness, pointing me to the future. Here and now, I give you my promise that my heart forever belongs only to you, these arms will only ever hold you and no one else."

"That's good enough for me," she whispered.

Larry felt her love, but he wanted the declaration. Before he could open his mouth, she beat him to it.

"It's been a long road, but I've finally found the love I sought," she touched the tip of his nose. "My dear good man, I love you with my whole heart. Now, do the right thing and make an honest woman of me or else I shall take it upon myself to do so."

And he laughingly placed a ring on her finger, this time a gold band with a small glittering diamond.

"Barbara Dorcas Coomb, once more I ask, will you do me the honour of agreeing to be my wife and put me out of my misery?"

"Yes Larry, yes I will," tears filled her eyes as he took her hand once again. "I really do love you," she declared, so grateful that she had found this man to love.

He drew her close, "I love you too, always and forever." And he meant it with his whole heart.

THANK YOU FOR CHOOSING A PUREREAD BOOK!

We hope you enjoyed the story, and as a way to thank you for choosing PureRead we'd like to send you this free book, and other fun reader rewards...

Click here for your free copy of Whitechapel Waif
PureRead.com/victorian

Thanks again for reading.
See you soon!

LOVE VICTORIAN ROMANCE?

If you enjoyed this story why not continue straight away with other books in our PureRead Victorian Romance library?

Read them all...

Orphan Christmas Miracle

An Orphan's Escape

The Lowly Maiden's Loyalty

Ruby of the Slums

The Dancing Orphan's Second Chance

Cotton Girl Orphan & The Stolen Man

Victorian Slum Girl's Dream

The Lost Orphan of Cheapside

Dora's Workhouse Child

Saltwick River Orphan

Workhouse Girl and The Veiled Lady

OUR GIFT TO YOU

AS A WAY TO SAY THANK YOU WE WOULD LOVE TO SEND YOU THIS BEAUTIFUL STORY FREE OF CHARGE.

Our Reader List is 100% FREE

Click here for your free copy of Whitechapel Waif

PureRead.com/victorian

At PureRead we publish books you can trust. Great tales without smut or swearing, but with all of the mystery and romance you expect from a great story.

Be the first to know when we release new books, take part in our fun competitions, and get surprise free books in your inbox by signing up to our Reader list.

As a thank you you'll receive an exclusive copy of Whitechapel Waif - a beautiful book available only to our subscribers...

Click here for your free copy of Whitechapel Waif

PureRead.com/victorian

Milton Keynes UK
Ingram Content Group UK Ltd.
UKHW011439120724
445583UK00022B/178

9 798648 591